LAIRD OF DRUMM

As joint heir to the Hebridean island of
Drumm, Ilona felt she had every right to
stay there—but the arrogant Kyle
Lachlan made it clear she was not
welcome. Why should he consider
himself the sole owner—and was it
Ilona's heart or her head that decided
her to stay put?

LAIRD OF
DRUMM

BY
CAROLINE CHARLES

MILLS & BOON LIMITED
15–16 BROOK'S MEWS
LONDON W1A 1DR

First published 1983

© Caroline Charles 1983

Australian copyright 1983

ISBN 0 263 10221 1

Set in Monophoto Times 11 on 11 pt.
07–0283 – 51144

*Made and printed in Great Britain by
Richard Clay (The Chaucer Press) Ltd.,
Bungay, Suffolk*

CHAPTER ONE

BEFORE she left King's Cross station, headed north for Scotland, Ilona bought some books to read on the journey, but once the train passed the unlovely London suburbs she was much too interested in watching the springtime scenery fly past, so the books remained unread. Besides, now that she had actually started her trip she was beginning to be tormented by doubts.

Her imagination ran ahead of her, to the Western Isles off the coast of Scotland, the Hebrides, and to a man she knew only by name— Kyle Lachlan. What would he be like, this co-heir of hers? A dour, grey-haired Scot with features weathered like his native landscape? That was how she imagined him. Certainly he would be unfriendly—his letter had been enough to demonstrate that.

If it hadn't been for that brusque letter, she might never have come on this journey. Legally she had a right to her half-share of the inheritance left by her great-uncle, but morally she had felt awkward about it, since she had never known Hamish McGregor. If her co-heir had been another relative she might well have forgone the inheritance altogether, but since he was only an employee she had felt sorry for her unknown great-uncle, who must have been a lonely man. For some reason he had wanted her to travel to the Isle of Drumm and stay there. It was her duty to respect his last wishes.

Even so, she had been vacillating until that letter came—a letter which virtually warned her off, offering to buy her share of Drumm rather than have her set foot on the place. *That* was what had finally tipped the scales.

Unfortunately, she had been so annoyed that she had decided not to warn Mr Lachlan of her arrival. Righteous indignation had seemed justified while she was safely at home, but now that she was on her way she wondered at the wisdom of her secrecy. Still, it was too late now to change her mind.

As the swift miles passed beneath the chuckling wheels of the train, she told herself sternly that, whatever Kyle Lachlan might think, she had every right to take at least a look at the Isle of Drumm.

Scotland in late April was ablaze with soft colours: acres of broom glowed yellow on hillsides above woods bursting with fresh green. Lochs showed rippling reflections of braes against the blue sky. Daffodils nodded in profusion across parkland around ancient houses, and rhododendron bushes budded in shades of violet, pink and blue. And always there were the mountains, craggy sage-green flanks lofting towards the arc of sky, some still tipped with snow while others looked blue with distance.

Reaching her destination on the coast, Ilona was enchanted by the stone houses painted in different pastel shades. In the crowded harbour, fishing boats lifted their masts as perches for clouds of scavenging gulls, while ferries and steamers ploughed to and fro across the Sound, connecting the mainland with the islands. She saw the misty Coolin Mountains rising majestic on the Isle of

Skye and her heart rose in answer. To her own surprise, she felt as though she was coming home at last.

The rich burr of Scottish voices reminded her vividly of her father, but when she asked about a boat to take her to the Isle of Drumm people unaccountably seemed suspicious. Her enquiries were greeted with shrugs, shaking heads and sidelong looks.

Temporarily baulked, Ilona took a room at a small inn by the harbour, where the landlady told here there was no way of getting to Drum apart from the boat which visited the island once a week to take supplies, and that didn't usually take passengers—especially not holidaymakers. Strangers of any kind, it seemed, were unwelcome on Drumm.

Ilona was about to protest that she was not a holidaymaker when an old man leaning in a doorway across the lobby caught her eye.

'Ye dinna want to go there, lassie,' he said darkly. 'Yon's no place for the likes of you.'

'But I do want to go there,' Ilona argued. 'There must be someone who would take me. Someone with a boat? I'd be glad to pay for the trip.'

The old man's eyes seemed to glimmer as he said drily, 'Ye'd pay, all richt, but I doubt you'd be happy aboot it. And neither would the man who was fool enough to take ye. The Laird'd skin ye both alive and fly your hides from the flagpole at Creag Mhor.'

'The Laird?' Ilona queried.

'Wisht, Dougal!' the landlady scoffed. 'Mr Lachlan's not as bad as all that. Away with you, man, and stop frightening the lassie. Will you sign the guest book, now, dearie?'

So Kyle Lachlan called himself Laird of Drumm, Ilona thought angrily. Laird, indeed! Had he forgotten that half the island had been left to her, if she decided to stay? Skin her alive, would he? Just let him try it!

She took up the pen and bent to sign her name, but hesitated and wrote 'Margaret South' instead of Ilona McGregor. The more she learned of Kyle Lachlan the more she wondered exactly what he was hiding out there on 'his' island. Better not to risk having him forewarned of her coming, just in case he took it into his head to stop her.

That night she slept fitfully in her bed at the inn, disturbed by the restless murmur of the sea and the wailing gulls, and she woke to find a grey mist lying across the harbour. After breakfast, she went out intending to make more enquiries about passage to Drumm, even if it meant waiting for the provision boat, but before she had gone a dozen steps along the cobbles a voice behind her called, 'Miss South?' and she turned to find the old man named Dougal peering at her.

'I might know someone who'd take ye out to the forbidden isle,' he muttered. 'Come wi' me.'

He led her away from the harbour, along a path which climbed a hill and wound down again to where a sea-loch poked its watery finger into the land. Here a youth dressed in oilskins was readying a small dinghy for sea and after some hurried conversation in Gaelic with the old man he turned to grin at Ilona.

'Want to be smuggled out to Drumm, do ye? It's not much of a day for it.'

Ilona glanced doubtfully at the mist which reduced visibility to a few hundred yards. The water swelled heavily, oily grey in the morning light. 'I wouldn't want you to take any chances.'

'What, me?' he laughed. 'I'm not such a fool. There's not a deal of wind, but it'll get us there. Besides, there's a lass on Drumm I've a mind to visit. It'll cost ye five pounds, mind. Five pounds for the round trip. Ye wouldn't want to be staying there, would ye?'

'Oh—no,' said Ilona. 'You mean, you want to leave now?'

'Aye, why not? Climb aboard and we'll be off. No one'll see us in this weather. We can be there and back before anyone knows we've left.'

Although Ilona had not planned to leave so precipitately, the idea appealed to her sense of adventure. She could go to Drumm, take a look at it, and come back without needing to meet Kyle Lachlan. Then, if she wished, she could send him word—either to warn him of her official arrival, or perhaps to accept his offer and tell him to keep his 'lump of rock'.

She had not realised the dinghy would sway so much under the spell of the light breeze that hardly stirred the mist, or that the sea would act like a switchback, tossing the boat high before dropping it into green troughs. Her stomach began to churn as they passed the nearer island, which slid past like a shadow through the fog.

'Hold tight!' her companion called as they rode another swell, and, 'Lean back now! Mind the boom!'

As the time passed Ilona became fascinated by the sight of the unbroken waves that slid past within inches of her hand, the only things visible except for grey mist and the lad who kept making fun of her landlubber's ignorance, making incomprehensible remarks in Gaelic before laughing uproariously and shouting to her to hold on as some new gyration rocked the boat. It was well over an hour before he pointed ahead and she saw another shadow looming through the mist.

'The Isle of Drumm!' he shouted.

It looked forbidding, cliffs rising sheer from the pounding waves whose tumult filled the air as the boat drew nearer. The dinghy appeared to be heading straight for that cliff, towards a mass of jagged black rocks where the waves dashed themselves into a million flecks of spume. Watching in alarm, Ilona saw the rocks come closer. She half rose in her seat, crying a warning, and at the same moment the boat turned away from danger. The young man laughed, then gasped in panic.

'Mind the boom!' he yelled. 'The boom!'

Something knocked against her back with a force that robbed her of breath. She was falling, falling, and chill water closed over her, causing a rushing in her ears. Her arms struck out wildly and as she came up she saw the boat moving away. The sea took her again, choking her. Then her head exploded with scarlet stars, her body rolled helplessly . . .

An iron band fastened round her waist. Someone's arm. She felt another body beside her, taking her in an upward surge. Light returned. Her head broke surface and she gulped gratefully at fresh air, aware of the strength of her rescuer as he supported her through the waves to a rocky shore where she stumbled and lay helpless, gasping for breath, her head whirling. Before she could get her thoughts in order she felt herself lifted as easily as if she were a doll, muscular arms giving her such a sense of security that she loosed her tenuous hold on consciousness and gave in to black limbo, trusting her safety to the unknown man who had rescued her.

She woke with a start, her heart thumping with alarm brought by that dream of drowning. With relief she realised that it had been a dream, but so vivid that her ears still rang with the cries of gulls.

A shudder ran through her as she opened her eyes, blinking in misty sunlight. For a moment she was disorientated. The morning sun never shone in her own room, nor did seagulls mew beyond her window.

The gulls were real!

Shocked back to full wakefulness, Ilona peered round in dismay at the unfamiliar room where she lay in bed. Heavy oak furniture lined the walls, and the sun struck through gold-coloured curtains which covered the window set in a curved wall. A curved wall, with a padded windowseat.

As she tried to sit up, pain lanced through her head and she sank back with a muffled groan. Memory returned. She really had been drowning. That explained her aching limbs and the soreness in her nose and throat. And there had been a man, a strong, capable man who had hauled her out of the sea and carried her ... to where? Where was this place?

She sat up very slowly, so as not to disturb the pain in her head. Carefully exploring her hair, she found a lump beneath the scalp that made her wince as she touched it. Her hair felt thick and sticky with salt, and with horror she realised she was totally naked beneath the sheets. Who had undressed her?

Holding her head still for fear it might fall off, Ilona climbed from the bed, taking the patchwork coverlet to wrap around herself toga-fashion. She drew aside the curtain, startling a gull that took flight from the windowsill to join his fellows in the air. The birds wheeled and dipped, their wings brilliant white against the backdrop of sunlit sky.

Ilona gasped as she realised how high her vantage point was, way above a sea-loch that stretched crookedly in front of her between hills whose steep flanks were clad in sage-green grass. Kneeling on the windowseat to be nearer the glass, she looked down to where the head of the loch met a rocky beach, from where gardens had been made on the hillside below her. Paths and steps climbed up past a waterfall, through sprays of bright blossoms and beds gay with flowers.

Most assuredly this could not be the Isle of Drumm, for it was hard to see this subtropical paradise as 'a slab of rock battered by Atlantic gales'. The tide must have swept her to some other island. Unless, of course, she had really drowned and was now in Heaven—but she dismissed that thought at once; the lump on her head and the stiffness of her muscles were all too real.

Behind her, the door-latch clicked, making her swing round and fling a hand to her head as a wave of dizziness swept her.

'Why, bairn!' a soft female voice addressed her. 'What are you doing out of your bed? You're not well enough to be up yet.'

Gentle hands urged her back to the softness of sheets, but Ilona clutched at her makeshift toga until it was firmly withdrawn and the blankets wrapped round her. She looked up into a rosy face with smiling blue eyes.

'Don't you worry about your modesty, my dearie,' the woman comforted. 'Who do you think undressed you?'

'You did?' Ilona breathed. Thank heaven for that!

'Of course I did, and I'm going to go on looking after you until you're well.' The woman busied herself straightening the bedcovers and replacing the coverlet with hands on which a wedding ring gleamed against work-worn fingers. A voluminous apron enveloped her plump figure, with sweater sleeves rolled up to the elbow, and her greying hair curled in a soft bun at her nape.

The bed tidy, she paused to smile down at Ilona's pale face. 'A bite of breakfast will do you the world of good. There's some porridge, then maybe you'd like a boiled egg, with some of my fresh bread.'

'It sounds lovely,' Ilona murmured, realising that she was hungry. 'It's very kind of you to go to so much trouble. I'm sorry——'

'Wisht!' the woman interrupted. 'Don't give it another thought, my dearie. You're welcome here. Besides,' with a laugh. 'You're not the first mermaid to be washed up on these shores.'

'Mermaid?' Ilona repeated.

'Aye, we have an old legend hereabouts. Your arrival reminded me of it. I'm Mrs McTavish, by the way. You rest yourself and I'll bring your breakfast.'

The latch clicked behind her and Ilona stared at the uneven ceiling, letting herself relax as she listened to the sounds around her. Seagulls cried raucously; waves murmured on the shores of the loch, and more distantly there came the faint thunder of breakers. Then a different noise made her glance towards the window in puzzlement.

Surely that was a helicopter? How odd and alien it sounded in this remote place as it buzzed overhead and came in to land somewhere nearby.

Returning with a tray, Mrs McTavish helped Ilona to sit up and brought a lacy bedjacket for her to wear.

'Your own clothes are almost dry,' she said. 'But I'll bring you a dressing gown for when you want to go to the bathroom. It's on the next landing down. We'd have put you in one of the main bedrooms, but we thought you'd be more peaceful up here.'

'It is very quiet,' Ilona agreed. 'Apart from the gulls. Do they always squawk so much?'

Mrs McTavish laughed. 'Aye, most of the time, but after a while you'll get used to it.'

Balancing the tray on her knees, Ilona dipped a spoon into the porridge, which had been liberally laced with cream and honey. It tasted delicious and slid down easily.

'I didn't realise how famished I was,' she admitted. 'But, come to think of it, I haven't eaten anything since . . . yesterday, was it?'

'Aye, dearie,' Mrs McTavish said with a look of concern. 'You've not really been with us, most of the time. We were in two minds whether to keep you here or take you to the hospital, but I've done a bit of nursing myself and you were so wet and cold the journey might have done more harm than good. But from the looks of you, you've not taken any permanent harm, though you could do with some feeding up.'

'Oh, I've always been this size,' said Ilona with a sigh. 'I don't feel too bad, really. When am I going to have the chance to thank your husband?'

'My husband?' Mrs McTavish said blankly.

'Wasn't it your husband who——' she was cut off when her companion laughed aloud, clapping her hands to her face as she looked merrily at her patient.

'Och, he'll not be very flattered when I tell him! No, lassie, it was not my husband. It was my employer—Mr Lachlan.'

Ilona bent her head over the last spoonful of porridge, hoping that her face would not betray the waves of heat and cold that swept through her. But Lachlan was a common enough name in Scotland. It was just coincidence. Oh, please let it be a coincidence!

'Are we . . .' she managed, 'on an island?'

'Aye—the Isle of Drumm. Why, I thought you would have known! It's lucky for you—and for that young fool Donald Ogg—that Mr Lachlan was by the shore yesterday. It was him brought you safe to Creag Mhor.'

Ilona felt the blood drain from her head, leaving her faint. What a fool she had been to arrive unexpectedly! Kyle Lachlan—her co-heir who didn't want her on Drumm—had been the one who dragged her from certain death on the rocks. What would he say when he found out who she was, and that she had tried to sneak on to the island to spite him?

Belatedly, she wished she had tackled the challenge in a more sensible manner instead of letting herself be carried away by a longing for adventure, by curiosity, and by sheer rebellion.

'You've been used to home comforts,' Aunt Zoe had scolded. 'You've been sheltered—heaven only knows how you'd have turned out if it hadn't been for me. You're too impulsive, Ilona—scatter-brained.'

Sighing to herself, Ilona had to admit that Aunt Zoe was probably right. Now she had landed herself in an impossibly embarrassing situation and the best thing to do would be to leave as soon as possible. At least no one here knew her real name.

When Mrs McTavish returned bringing a soft-boiled brown egg, buttered bread fingers and a pot of tea, Ilona introduced herself as 'Margaret South', but when she mentioned her desire to leave the island the housekeeper looked horrified.

'Leave? What, today? Why, Miss South, you're not well enough to go yet, even if there was a boat. The steamer won't be calling here for another three days. Besides, it's grand for me to have you here. I'll enjoy looking after you. I see little enough of my own daughter—she lives in Aberdeen. Her husband's a diver with the oil rigs.'

Disconsolately, Ilona finished her breakfast, enjoying the golden-yolked egg and the strong tea despite her feeling of being trapped. When the boat came she would scurry back home and put the whole thing down to experience.

Wrapped in an enormous towelling robe, which obviously belonged to Mrs McTavish, she ventured out on to the narrow landing from where a circular stair wound downwards, lit by a narrow window. There was a view over the leaded roofs of the castle to the hill behind, a steep clifflike head with rocky promontories. On the landing below, Ilona discovered the promised bathroom, which though antiquated provided all the necessary offices, including a shower beneath which she washed off the salt stickiness, being careful of the lump on her head.

When she emerged with her hair lying damply

round her shoulders, the silence of the house drew her down a further flight of curving stairs, to a gallery which opened out on to a huge hall. She stole silently, on bare feet, to the balustrade, and looked down into the panelled room below. Chairs and settees stood grouped round rugs laid on a gleaming parquet floor, and in a vast fireplace logs were laid ready to be lit. Around the walls, heavy-framed pictures looked down on brassware and leather, two crossed swords hung in tasselled scabbards, and a stag's head stared balefully.

Only the heavy tick-tock of a long-case clock disturbed the silence, and though she felt like an intruder Ilona reminded herself of her great-uncle's will. She was joint heir to this property, if she chose to claim it. No wonder Kyle Lachlan wanted it for himself. And as for his description of the island as bleak and dreary ... he had deliberately lied!

Bolstered by indignation, Ilona glanced along the gallery, where more rooms led off, before making for the stairs. The robe was long on her, going nearly twice round and fastened by a tie belt, but it was a perfect cover-all if someone should happen to appear. However, no sound came to her ears as she crept down the stairs, intent on exploration.

The parquet felt cold to her feet, then she stepped on to the soft wool rug, running a hand along a deeply-buttoned leather settee, while her lips tightened at the thought of Kyle Lachlan's daring to tell her to stay away.

She discovered a big dining room complete with banqueting table and carved chairs, a smaller sitting rom, and a morning room. Moving on, she reached a door in the corner of the hall.

She was surprised to find herself in a small office cramped with cabinets and bookshelves. On the desk, papers lay scattered. Carefully closing the door behind her, Ilona tiptoed round the desk and began to glance through the documents, seeing with surprise that a good many of them appeared to be scientific reports, maps and charts, full of incomprehensible jargon, which made her wonder afresh just what Kyle Lachlan was up to.

About to retreat, she paused as she caught sight of a framed photograph half hidden behind a rolled map. She picked it up and looked curiously at the young woman whose image smiled back at her—a stunningly beautiful young woman with raven hair and dark eyes. Lachlan's daughter? she wondered.

That was when the door opened.

Ilona whirled, clasping the photograph to her breast, the colour draining from her face as she stared in confusion at the man who had paused with his hand on the doorknob, himself startled by the sight of her.

He seemed to fill the doorway, so tall and broad-shouldered that she could not have passed him even if she had had the courage to try. Hair of a rich chestnut red lay in windblown curls about a face that seemed all angles, with strong brows, aquiline nose and a jawline that jutted threateningly as he recovered from his surprise and discovered that he had interrupted her in the act of snooping—at least, that must be how it seemed to him, Ilona thought.

Frozen with horror and embarrassment, she hung there, clutching the photograph, green eyes wide in her pale face, her hair a tousled shower of gold and her slender figure enveloped in the

ridiculous dressing gown. She was shamedly aware
of the sight she must present, and though she ran
her tongue nervously across dry lips her throat
would utter no sound.

'Miss South,' the man said in a low voice edged
with disgust, not moving from his stance by the
doorway.

'I——' Ilona croaked. 'I was ... looking for
Mrs McTavish. I wondered if my clothes were dry.'
The lies made her even more ashamed of herself.

His lip curled slightly. 'Really? Then please
carry on with your search. Maybe Mrs McTavish
is hiding under the desk, or in one of the drawers.
Or did you think she might be squeezed into that
picture-frame?'

Face flaming now, Ilona hurriedly bent forward
to replace the photograph, realising as she did so
that the loose top of the robe was gaping open.
She threw up a hand to draw the lapels together
and straightened herself, meeting the coldest and
greyest pair of eyes she had ever seen.

'I'm sorry,' she muttered. 'You're right, I was
being nosey. I'm always being told I'm too nosey
for my own good.'

'You might remember what curiosity did to the
cat,' the man said levelly.

'Yes, I—I'm sorry.' What else could she say? If
only he would move and let her escape from this
waking nightmare. 'Are you ... are you Mr
Lachlan?'

'I am,' he agreed with a slight bow which only
seemed to accentuate his height when he lifted his
head again. He was enormous, Ilona thought
fearfully. Long legs were clad in close-fitting cords
and a navy-blue sweater did little to disguise the
muscular breadth of his torso. No wonder he had

carried her from the sea with such ease. He was twice the size she was.

'I haven't thanked you for what you did,' she babbled. 'I'm so grateful. It was a stupid thing to do, standing up in the boat. If you hadn't been there . . .' She stopped herself, one hand caught at her throat to hold the robe. She was intensely aware that beneath it she was naked. Defenceless— that was the way she felt in the company of this huge redheaded man who regarded her with an ironic twist to his lips.

'If I hadn't been there,' he completed her thought, 'you wouldn't be snooping round my study. And Donald Ogg would have had you on his conscience for the rest of his life.'

Ilona swallowed hard, wishing her head didn't hurt so much. 'Donald Ogg?'

'Your gallant boatman,' he informed her with a trace of sarcasm. 'It wasn't enough for the young fool to bring a stranger—and without a life-jacket—no, he had to show off, too, and nearly killed you. He fancies himself master of these waters, but one of these days he'll regret it. The sea will not be mocked.'

'No, I suppose not,' she agreed feebly, thinking that he had a beautiful voice if nothing else, rich and deep with a flavour of the Highlands in its inflection. 'And I—I was stupid to have been a party to——'

'Yes, you were. Stupid and irresponsible.' His tone roughened and anger glittered again in the grey eyes. 'But to judge by present performance, that's in character.'

She caught her breath, stiffening her spine to look him in the eye. 'How dare you speak to me in that way?'

'How dare I?' His brows came down to shadow pale cold eyes and he took a step towards her, making Ilona flinch away. 'I might ask you the same. How dare you come uninvited to my island and then make yourself free around my house?'

His island? *His* house? Ilona's temper blazed at his arrogance. 'I admit to curiosity,' she retorted. 'But I've touched nothing nor looked at anything that wasn't already on display. I was looking round the house, that's all.'

'All?' he repeated. 'Then you must have been raised to be ill-mannered. Is this the way you show your gratitude? If I'd known you were a spy——'

'I'm not!' she gasped.

'Then you're giving a good impression of it! Go back to your room and stay there until you're invited to leave it.'

He stood aside, leaving the path through the door free. Tossing back her hair, Ilona began to march round the desk, only to have the robe catch on a splinter of wood and detain her, at the same time displaying one slim bare leg for her adversary's diversion. She saw his eyes widen momentarily before she tugged the robe free and wrapped its skirts securely around her, her head beginning to thump. With as much dignity as her quivering nerves would allow, she continued towards the door.

'Well, one thing's for sure,' Kyle Lachlan said as she came abreast of him. 'You're certainly not a mermaid.'

Ilona stopped, tilting her chin defiantly to look at him. 'Did I appear to have a tail yesterday?'

The light in his eyes had changed, no longer cold but glinting with sardonic amusement that infuriated her. 'I was too occupied to take much notice,' he said. 'You were as wet and limp as a dead herring. But you wouldn't have been the first mermaid to be landed here. These islands are full of fishy legends.'

'So your housekeeper told me,' she said, aching from the strain of holding herself erect. If only she hadn't been barefooted she might have come up to his chin; as it was, she felt petite beside him. He towered over her in much the same way the crag towered behind the castle, both of them equally impervious.

'Did she, indeed?' he drawled. 'And what other secrets have you prised out of her?'

'What other secrets are there?'

'That's for me to know and you to wonder about—until the boat comes.'

She wanted to say something else, but the thoughts wouldn't come in the right order. Her head ached spitefully and suddenly she felt faint, her senses swimming dizzily. She muttered, 'Excuse me,' and hurried to the sanctuary of the tower room.

Taking off the towelling robe, she slid back beneath sheets that felt cool and welcoming as sleep beckoned her into its healing folds. From now on she would follow Mrs McTavish's advice and stay in bed—not least to save herself the intense displeasure of meeting Kyle Lachlan again. Hateful, horrible man! Just who did he think he was?

CHAPTER TWO

As she dozed, drifting in and out of sleep, memories swirled disjointedly through her mind, troubling her. Only a few weeks before, the Isle of Drumm had been a half-mythical place remembered from childhood stories. Her father had often told her amusing tales of his unsociable Uncle Hamish, who lived alone on a remote Scottish island and did not welcome visitors, not even his own kin. Great-uncle Hamish had been something of a joke.

Then the stories had stopped, because when Ilona was eight her parents had been killed in a motorway pile-up and over the years Great-uncle Hamish and his island had faded into the back of her memory. She had all but forgotten them as she concentrated on the task of growing up.

After her parents' death, she had been given a home by her mother's sister, Zoe South, in a house in Surrey, where Ilona grew up in company with her cousin Marianne. Aunt Zoe had not been unkind, but she had never allowed Ilona to forget how grateful she ought to be.

'It's too bad of you to be so wicked!' she would exclaim whenever Ilona committed some minor childhood sin. 'If it hadn't been for me you'd have been sent to an orphanage, and how would you have liked that? I can still send you there if you don't behave, you know.'

Although Aunt Zoe, who was herself widowed,

had been left with ample money, she was frugal enough to make Ilona wear Marianne's cast-off clothing. None of it fitted properly since the older girl was bigger-boned, almost lumpish against Ilona's slightness—a fact for which Marianne never forgave her cousin. Another cause for resentment was the difference in their looks: Marianne was dark, sallow-skinned, and could at best be called handsome, while Ilona grew slender and curvaceous, her hair golden-blonde and her eyes green as sea-pools. Aunt Zoe, offended by her niece's good looks, lost no opportunity to call attention to her small imperfections and in consequence Ilona was never tempted to vanity. On the contrary, she thought herself quite unattractive.

Even when she left school and took a job in an office there was little respite from Aunt Zoe's nagging. Ilona was expected to give a large proportion of her salary in return for board and lodging.

'It's about time I had some recompense for all the years I've supported that child,' Zoe South remarked to a neighbour, unaware that Ilona was within earshot.

When Marianne married and had a baby, Ilona was called in to baby-sit two or three times a week. The rest of her spare time was taken up with housework, since Aunt Zoe had recently become a victim of 'nerves' which prevented her from doing much apart from sitting around reading and entertaining friends to coffee mornings and afternoon teas, which gave her further opportunities to complain about her niece's short-comings.

Then the worst happened: because of the

economic slump, Ilona lost her job as a secretary
and found herself at home most of the time, at her
aunt's beck and call every waking moment.
Though she bit her tongue often to save
arguments, since she knew her aunt to be an
unhappy woman, as the winter dragged on she
began to feel that she would go mad if something
didn't happen—some change in the routine, or
some adventure, however small . . .

On a day in early March, she had leaned by the
window in the cold light of dawn, blearily staring
at the frost which filled each beech-leaf cup on the
brown hedge. Really she could have done with a lie-
in that morning since she had been up until two
a.m. baby-sitting while Marianne and her husband
went off to a dinner-dance, but she had had to
drag herself out of bed as soon as the alarm rang
because Aunt Zoe liked a morning cup of tea in
bed—'To help me start the day slowly.'

She prepared a tray with cup and saucer, milk
and sweeteners, adding a plate of Rich Tea biscuits
and a small steaming pot of tea, and went out into
the hall just as the letterbox clacked and a spatter
of envelopes landed on the mat.

'Ilona?' her aunt's imperious voice came from
one of the rooms above. 'Ilona, was that the
postman? Bring the letters up to me at once.'

'Just coming, Aunt Zoe,' Ilona replied, setting
the tray down on the hall table before bending to
scoop up the letters without troubling to see who
they were for. Straightening, she swept back her
tumbled blonde hair, paused to cover a luxurious
yawn and, with a shiver, climbed the stairs with
the mail on the tray.

Her aunt sat in bed wearing a thick crocheted
jacket over a flannelette nightgown, her tightly-

permed hair already combed and a smudge of lipstick brightening her thin lips.

'You look terrible,' she told Ilona. 'Couldn't you even comb that mane of yours? It looks awful. I suppose you've only just got up, since you came in so late.'

'I didn't disturb you, did I?' Ilona said. 'I tried not to make any noise.'

'Everything disturbs me,' her aunt replied grouchily. 'You know what a light sleeper I am. Really you should have stayed at Marianne's as she suggested. Then you could have got to bed at a reasonable time instead of crawling in with the dawn.'

'Perhaps you're right,' Ilona said, containing a sigh as she handed her aunt the letters and began to pour tea. There were times when she felt she could never do anything right. If she had stayed at Marianne's house her aunt would have complained bitterly about being left alone. Anyway, she never felt welcome at Marianne's.

'These are for you,' said Zoe South, handing her two envelopes. 'I only hope one of them is the offer of a job. You can't go on forever sitting around twiddling your thumbs.'

Ilona took the letters, echoing her aunt's hope. Household chores were hardly 'twiddling her thumbs', but she would be relieved to have a real job again, if only to allow her an escape from the lodge during office hours.

However, the first letter was yet another 'Sorry, but the position has been filled'. She had lost count of the number of those she had received over the past few months, and she refolded it with a sigh, fully expecting the second envelope to contain a similar message. But it was embossed with the name of a firm of solicitors in London—a firm to which she did not remember making application for a post.

With a frown, she tore it open and scanned the single sheet of paper. It came from a man named Harrison, who regretted to inform her of the death of her great-uncle Hamish McGregor but believed she might be interested to know she had been mentioned in his will.

'Well?' her aunt demanded. 'Is it good news?'

'I'm not sure,' said Ilona. 'See for yourself.'

Aunt Zoe read the letter twice, her brow corrugated. 'Hamish McGregor? There must be some mistake. I've never heard of him.'

'My father's family did come from Scotland,' Ilona reminded her. 'I do seem to remember him talking about an Uncle Hamish, but I was never sure if he was real or just a comic figure of Dad's imagination.'

'Uncle Hamish . . . Why, yes, I do believe you're right. He was a bit odd, wasn't he? A hermit, or something.' Zoe South's eyes began to gleam as if she scented profit. 'In that case, of course you must keep this appointment. If you're the beneficiary in a will . . . Why don't I come with you? A day up in London would do us both good. It's just what we need to bring us out of our end-of-the-winter doldrums.'

'Are you sure you're well enough?' Ilona asked.

'Oh, yes. Yes, I think I could manage it, even if I do suffer afterwards. Besides, I can't let you go alone. One hears of such strange things happening in London these days.'

Well aware of what was causing her aunt's eagerness, Ilona said, 'He probably hasn't left me anything much, you know. A keepsake, maybe. I don't remember hearing that he was rich.'

'Probably not, but you never know. Some of these recluses are rolling in money—look at Howard Hughes.'

Ilona bit her lip to prevent herself from laughing aloud. Aunt Zoe's imagination had run riot. Howard Hughes, indeed! Most likely there would be a bundle of old clothes and maybe a watch. Still, a day in London might be fun.

On the appointed day, she and her aunt went up to town by train, leaving behind the winter-bare trees of the wooded Surrey hills as they came to the sprawling suburbs of the great city. A taxi took them to Selfridges, where they had coffee, and from there it was a brief walk through windy streets to the solicitor's office.

In the secretary's office, Mr Harrison met them and shook hands, regarding Ilona with interest. Aunt Zoe turned all pinched and sniffy when the portly solicitor practically ordered her to stay with his secretary and have a cup of coffee while he took Ilona into his inner sanctum.

'But I'm her aunt,' Zoe South protested. 'I've brought her up. I've a right to know——'

'I expect she'll tell you, in due course,' Mr Harrison replied, leading Ilona firmly away and closing the door on her aunt's outraged face.

It was a quiet room double-glazed against the hum of traffic, with thick nets across the window and a gas fire making the air dry. Books lined the wall, with filing cabinets and shelves crammed with documents, the whole pervaded by the aroma of stale tobacco. Amused by the way he had dealt with her aunt, Ilona sank down in an armchair as Mr Harrison filled a pipe, watching her all the while through half-moon glasses which gave him the air of a friendly goblin.

'So you're Ilona Margaret McGregor,' he said, perching on a corner of his desk. 'My letter came as a surprise, I dare say.'

'You could put it like that,' Ilona agreed, laughing a little self-consciously. 'I'd forgotten about my father's Uncle Hamish. I never met him—I suppose I thought he'd died years ago. He must have been a very old man.'

The solicitor laid a match to his pipe, nodding at her through fronds of smoke. 'Nearly ninety. And you weren't the only one who never met him. From what I can gather, he was something of a recluse. But as I said in my letter, I'm acting on behalf of my associate, Andrew McKay, who has his office in Edinburgh. He was your great-uncle's legal adviser. I didn't myself have the pleasure of making the acquaintance of Mr McGregor. However, I do have a copy of the will, if you'd care to see it.'

'Perhaps you could just tell me the gist,' Ilona said swiftly.

Mr Harrison chuckled. 'Don't want to wade through reams of legal jargon, eh? All those heretofores and whereases. I can't say I blame you.' Sorting through some papers on his desk, he took up an important-looking document and scanned it. 'There are several small bequests, as you probably appreciate. To friends and so on. But the bulk of the estate has been left jointly— between you and Mr Lachlan.'

The bulk of the estate? she thought, perplexed, but since the phrase didn't bring anything to mind she grasped at the one tangible thing she could understand. 'Mr Lachlan? Who's he?'

'Ah, he was your great-uncle's factor—his estate manager.'

There was that word 'estate' again. But if half of it had been left to an employee then it couldn't be much. Ilona had begun to feel as though she were dreaming. Nothing about this meeting was as she had expected it to be.

'I'm not sure how your great-uncle made his fortune,' the solicitor was saying. 'But his stocks and shares provide a considerable income which is used to maintain the island—the island being the property part of the estate.'

He said more, but Ilona's mind had seized up with shock. Considerable income? Island? Had she heard correctly? Suddenly the room seemed unbearably warm and the pipe-smoke stung her eyes.

Regarding her with concern, the solicitor noted her pallor and the way she pulled at her long honey-gold hair with nervous fingers. She seemed very young for her twenty-one years and he wondered if she would understand the significance of what he had to say next.

'There is a condition,' he told her softly. 'Before you can claim your half-share, you must live on the island for six full months. The place meant a great deal to your great-uncle and he was anxious to leave it in the hands of someone who would care for it as he did.'

'Where . . . where is this island?' Ilona faltered.

'Off the west coast of Scotland, in the Hebrides. I gather it's a remote place, not to everyone's taste. Mr McGregor wanted you to get to know it, and its people, and if you can stand it for six months then you're fit to own half of it. At least, that appears to have been what was in his mind.'

Ilona struggled to take in this astonishing news.

She had expected only some small bequest—a sum of money, or an heirloom—but an island! It was too much to take in all at once.

'What is it called?' she asked.

'The Isle of Drumm. It's only a small place—a few crofts, some fishing ... Your great-uncle's house is called Creag Mhor.'

The names alone set Ilona's blood racing. The Isle of Drumm—it conjured dreams, calling to her all the more strongly because of its mystery. And Creag Mhor—she imagined the words spoken in her father's soft Scots accent. Great-uncle Hamish had flung out a challenge which she, Ilona Margaret McGregor, would gladly accept. It was just the sort of adventure she had been longing for.

'You're surely not thinking of going?' her aunt said on the train home to Surrey. 'What on earth would you do with an island? It sounds a godforsaken place. I know that Skye and all those other places are popular for holidays, but nobody in his right mind actually lives there, unless he has the misfortune to be born there. It's all covered in mist half the time, even in summer. In winter it must be appalling—no doctors, no mod. cons. Like living in the Middle Ages. Obviously your great-uncle must have had a peculiar sense of humour. He must have known you wouldn't go. Are you sure the will is legal?'

'Perfectly legal,' said Ilona, a dreamy look in her sea-green eyes. 'Of course I shall go, if only to see the place. I *must* go, Aunt Zoe. This is my chance to see the place where my ancestors came from—the Isle of Drumm. Creag Mhor.'

Her aunt shuddered. 'It sounds a heathenish place to me. And what do you imagine I shall do without you?'

'You can always go to stay with Marianne,' Ilona suggested. 'Little Gary's at a lovely stage, just learning to walk, and the spring weather will soon be here. Besides, if I don't go, I can't make any claims under the terms of the will.'

That stopped her aunt's protests. Zoe South was not one to forgo a chance of money. For Ilona, it wasn't the fortune that mattered; she didn't really expect to stay on Drumm for six months, she just wanted to see it.

But before she had entirely made up her mind what to do, another letter arrived at the lodge—a rather brusque letter which read:

'Dear Miss McGregor, I understand that you have been informed of the terms of your great-uncle's will, and I thought I would write to add a postscript of my own. You ought to know that Drumm is not everyone's idea of heaven, being little more than a slab of rock battered by Atlantic gales, where living is hard. We have no regular passenger boat and few facilities, no hotels or shops. To save you the trouble of bringing yourself all the way here on what would probably prove to be a wild-goose chase, I have a proposition to make.

'I hereby offer to buy your share of the island, in order to respect your legal rights as Hamish McGregor's only relative. We could leave our lawyers to decide on a fair price, but I trust you will agree that a sum of money, without strings, is preferable to six months in exile on a lonely lump of granite. Even if you chose to come here as your great-uncle wished, a half-share in Drumm will not make you a rich woman. You would probably find it more like an albatross round your neck. Sincerely, Kyle Lachlan.'

'If I were you,' her aunt said, 'I'd accept this offer. The place sounds just as awful as I feared. And we could use a nice little nest-egg.'

Ilona silently noted that 'we', and sighed at the thought of arguments to come. If she had her way, the money would provide her with a flat of her own, where she would no longer be made to feel an unwelcome, but useful, member of her aunt's household.

'I'd still like to see the island first,' she replied. 'I think I will go, just for a week or so, and then Mr Lachlan can have the place to himself. We can talk about financial arrangements while I'm there.'

Her aunt grumbled a good deal, but was mollified by the thought of the nest-egg which would eventually come after Ilona had satisfied her curiosity.

Having made up her mind, Ilona immediately began to make arrangements for her trip to Scotland. She sensed a mystery which only increased her determination to go, and that was why she had omitted to warn her co-heir of her plans.

All she wanted to do was show him there was one McGregor left, and that he couldn't have everything his own way. Once she had shown herself and found out why he had warned her off then she would tell him she had no desire to intrude on his lonely retreat. She would accept his offer and depart, with honours even.

At least, that was what she had thought before she arrived. As it had turned out, everything had gone wrong: now she could not announce her identity without appearing to be a liar, and she had a feeling that Kyle Lachlan would not sit still and listen to involved explanations and excuses.

Oh dear, why hadn't she *told* him she was coming?

'I came up a while ago,' the housekeeper told her, arriving with a lunch tray, 'but you were asleep. What did you think you were up to, going wandering like that? Why, dearie, if you'd collapsed I'd never have known. Still, you've a wee bit more colour now. I expect the sleep did you good.'

Ilona wondered how much Kyle Lachlan had told her of her exploits downstairs, but the housekeeper's attitude remained friendly and concerned, so perhaps he hadn't said he had caught Ilona prying. But Creag Mhor *was* part of the inheritance and though neither Kyle Lachlan nor Mrs McTavish knew it, she had every right to look around the lovely old place.

She was finishing her lunch when the helicopter returned again, droning overhead to land somewhere beside the castle.

'Helicopter?' queried Mrs McTavish when she came to fetch the tray. 'Aye, dearie, that'll be Mr Lachlan coming back,' and she left the room before Ilona had time to ask more questions. So the island boasted a helicopter for the use of its Laird, did it?

Feeling drowsy again, she took off the bedjacket she had donned and tossed it aside before settling down in the comfort of the bed. Perhaps after another nap she might feel well enough to ask for her clothes, though how she would manage in the same outfit for three days was problematical. Maybe she ought to stay in bed, out of Kyle Lachlan's way, until the boat came. Oh, that man! That devious, lying . . .

She sat up in alarm as the door crashed open and he appeared as if her thoughts had brought him. Frantically clutching the blankets in front of her, Ilona stared in disbelief as she saw that he was carrying her cases, which he dumped at the end of the bed.

'How on earth . . .?' she began.

'No one can accuse me of being a bad host,' he broke in, standing arms akimbo with that tousled red head on one side. 'Your belongings, milady. Now you've no more excuse for tripping around in that indecent robe.'

'Since it belongs to Mrs McTavish,' Ilona said frostily, 'I hardly thinks it's indecent.'

His gaze swept her boldly, making her aware of her rumpled hair, bare arms and shoulders. 'On Mrs McTavish it may be sensible and homely, no doubt allied with a flanelette night gown,' he said patiently. 'On you, with nothing but you inside it, it was indecent.'

Ilona's cheeks grew scarlet, making her eyes bright as she glared green sparks at him. 'If you were a gentleman, you wouldn't have noticed!'

'I'd have had to be dead, or in my dotage, not to notice,' he replied. 'Since I'm neither, you'd better think twice before you parade around my house in a state of undress again. We're a little short of women on this island and I might take it into my head to demand recompense for my trouble.'

His eyes seemed to probe even through the blankets, and Ilona felt he was quite capable of carrying out this threat. She slid further down into the bed, afraid of his greater strength. 'You wouldn't dare!'

'Wouldn't I! I advise you not to tempt me, my little whey-faced mermaid. There are some who would say I had every right to do as I please with you. If someone saves a life, then that life belongs to him—haven't you heard of that tradition?'

'We're not in the Dark Ages!' Ilona exclaimed.

'No.' He spoke the word softly, lowering his craggy head to look at her through his eyelashes. 'We're on the Isle of Drumm, and I'm the master here. I advise you not to forget it.'

Without haste, he turned on his heel and strode out, closing the door softly. The faint click of the latch was somehow more unnerving than a slam would have been.

Ilona was half dozing when, some time later, Mrs McTavish crept in and began to unpack the cases. Her movements about the room disturbed Ilona, who lifted herself on to one elbow to ask, 'How did Mr Lachlan know where to find my things?'

'Donald Ogg told him.'

'The lad who brought me here?'

'The same.' Mrs McTavish's voice sounded gruff with disapproval. 'Mr Lachlan recognised the boat. He knew where young Donald was headed—off courting in the village, though the lassie's father'll take a belt to him if he catches him.'

'And he told Mr Lachlan about my staying at the inn?'

'He did. When Mr Lachlan sets out to get information there's few can deny him, especially not that young scallawag. He's been told often enough to steer clear of Drumm, but he hasn't the sense to take heed. Or maybe it's a case of forbidden fruit being sweetest. Young Donald's daft enough for anything.'

Why, Ilona wondered, should Donald Ogg be barred from the island? The more she heard, the more intrigued she became.

The housekeeper reached to put the empty cases on top of the wardrobe, saying, 'I'm going to make a cup of tea now, then later maybe you'll feel well enough to join Mr Lachlan for dinner.'

Dismay made Ilona feel giddy again, but before she could find a reply Mrs McTavish had turned, partially offbalance, and her elbow caught the books lying on the tallboy, sending them thudding to the floor.

'Oh, clumsy!' she chided herself, bending to retrieve the books. 'I hope I haven't damaged them—no, they're all right. You like to read, do you?'

'When I have the chance,' said Ilona. 'I bought those to read on the train, but I was much too interested in watching the views.'

Mrs McTavish cast her a sidelong look, said, 'Aye, well, you'll maybe have time to read them while you're here. There's not much of a night-life on Drumm,' and departed.

Later she brought Ilona a cup of tea, but seemed disinclined to chat, saying only that dinner would be served just after sunset, if Ilona cared to come down. She was almost brusque, but Ilona assumed she was busy and thought no more about it—she had more important things to ponder.

During the day, the thought of flight had seemed less and less inviting. Why should she go away when her great-uncle had virtually invited her to come? If she did leave she would never dare come back and admit to her deception, but the mysteries of Drumm had become much too intriguing to leave unsolved. Besides, she had a perfect right to be here—as much right as Kyle Lachlan. There was really only one thing for it— she had to admit to her real identity and establish her rights as Hamish McGregor's joint heir.

Feeling much better for an afternoon's rest, she slipped down to the bathroom and took another shower, beginning to relish what lay ahead. What could Kyle Lachlan do to her? Skin her alive, as old Dougal had sworn he might? Let him do his worst. Ilona McGregor, now that she felt more herself, would prove a match for him. Tonight he was in for a surprise.

She made up her face carefully, accentuating her eyes and high cheekbones, and brushed her hair until it shone. Liberally spraying on perfume, she slipped into a dress of primrose cotton embroidered in darker yellow around the broad waistband and on the tiny sleeves. It had a Chinese-style top, little stand-up collar, and a flaring skirt that reached just below her knees. Aunt Zoe had loved it, but Ilona thought it a little prim; however, it would do for this evening, since she needed no more sexy overtures from that redheaded giant.

Surveying the result in the mirror, she pulled a face at her reflection. Tonight she would have liked to be beautiful, but as Aunt Zoe had told her so often, nature was not always kind. Nature had given Ilona a curious tip-tilted nose sprinkled with pale freckles. 'Like a pixie,' Aunt Zoe had said. 'And your mouth's too big, unfortunately. As for your figure—it's such a pity flat bosoms are in fashion.'

Ilona sighed ruefully at the rounded outline revealed by the tight top of the dress, seeing only the minor imperfections which her aunt had been so careful to point out and not the overall effect, which had made many a man feel hot around the collar, if only she had known it. Still, it wasn't too bad. She felt confident enough to face Kyle

Lachlan and that was really all that mattered. It was not her intention to seduce him. Heavens— him! The very thought made her laugh, a little uncertainly.

Wearing high-heeled sandals, she glided down the winding stairs and emerged soundlessly on the carpeted gallery. For a moment she paused in the shadows, her heart beginning to beat unsteadily at the unnerving sight that waited for her in the great hall below.

Wall-lights glowed softly around the big room, leaving pools of shadow against which the fire burned brightly. And in front of that fire, feet planted apart, stood Kyle Lachlan, wearing the full formal dress of the Highlands—close-fitting velvet jacket over a white shirt and frilled jabot, with a kilt in a dark tartan, its deep pleats almost reaching the tops of thickknit socks. Against the forest green of his jacket the firelight accentuated the redness of his hair, making him look savage, like something out of Scottish myth, every inch of him hard and masculine. Ilona wondered if he had donned that costume to prove a point—to drive home the fact that he was master here. Laird of Drumm!

Laird of half of Drumm! she amended her own thought angrily. Who did he think he was, to lord it at Creag Mhor? He was no kin to Hamish McGregor, only his estate manager, yet to look at him one would have thought he was the last of some proud line of Highland chieftains.

When she moved towards the stairs he looked up, watching with veiled eyes as she came slowly down, one small hand resting on the polished banister, her head up and the pale yellow skirt flirting round her knees unconsciously drawing attention to shapely calves and trim ankles. She heard the measured ticking of the big old clock, the spitting of the logs, and her own pulse beat too fast in her throat.

At last she stepped down on to the parquet floor and paused there, wishing there was more light so that she could see his expression clearly, but his face was masked in shadow.

Suddenly aware of how dangerous the slippery parquet could be to high heels, Ilona walked carefully to the edge of the nearest rug and stopped, her chin lifted in a determined fashion.

'Mr Lachlan . . .'

He bowed briefly, mockingly, and the firelight glinted on the handle of a dirk tucked into one sock. Barbaric! she thought. But she had to concede that he looked magnificent—arrogantly proud and entirely male.

'My name,' she said slowly and clearly, 'is not South. I'm Ilona Margaret McGregor.'

Behind the tall, dark figure a log cracked and shifted, sending a shower of sparks up the chimney. Ilona's taut nerves twitched, but Kyle Lachlan remained still and silent as if waiting for her to go on.

'Did you hear what I said?' she asked more loudly. 'I'm Hamish McGregor's great-niece. His heir.'

'Joint heir.' He said it flatly, with not the least trace of emotion.

'That's what I meant! I didn't intend to deceive you. What happened . . . it was a mistake. I was confused, not myself.'

'You mean you lost your memory?'

'No, of course I don't!' She took a deep breath, trying to calm her screaming nerves. Why did he manage to make her feel as if she were totally in the wrong? He couldn't have done better if he had staged this whole scene himself—she standing in the light while his own face looked enigmatic in the shadows, though she fancied she saw the grey eyes glimmer.

'You don't seem surprised,' she commented, cursing the nervous hoarseness of her voice.

'Should I be?' the maddeningly-cool reply came. 'Did you think Mrs McTavish would fail to tell me?'

'Mrs McTavish couldn't have known!'

'Oh, come, Miss McGregor, don't take me for a fool. She saw your books—the books in which you had written your name very clearly.'

Books? Ilona swayed, a hand to her head. What a fool she had been not to realise the books might betray her! 'Always write your name in a book as soon as you buy it,' was Aunt Zoe's maxim, 'otherwise it will get lost, if someone borrows it.' And good little Ilona had done as she was told, brainwashed into writing her name on each shiny new fly-leaf without really thinking about it.

'I didn't realise . . .' she murmured.

Two huge strides brought him to stand before her, his expression all too clear now—grim, raging fury. He towered over her, glowering like some murderous Visigoth. 'Of course you realised! Why else did you decide you'd better confess right away?'

'Because I thought it was best to be honest!'

'Honest? Don't play the innocent with me, Miss McGregor. You knew very well what you were doing. I had my suspicions when they told me on the mainland how eager you'd been to get to Drumm, but I refused to believe a relative of

Hamish's would be so devious.'

'It wasn't devious!' Ilona argued. 'It just happened. I *was* confused. I lied because I was so ashamed of being found out.'

'I thought so. You were afraid I might guess that you came here to spy on me. You thought you could sneak on to Drumm without my knowing, and poke your toffee nose into my affairs, and peek and pry . . .'

Ilona threw back her head, glaring up at him. 'They're my affairs, too—a fact which you conveniently keep forgetting. And what is it I might have discovered, Mr Lachlan? What are you afraid of?'

He withdrew a little, the rage turning to ice-cold disdain. 'I'm afraid of nothing. There's nothing here that you couldn't have seen—if you had come openly and honestly. One thing I do know—if Hamish McGregor had been alive to witness this he'd have thrown you back into the sea sooner than let you stay here. He'd have been disgusted to acknowledge you as his kin!'

CHAPTER THREE

INTO the singing silence, Mrs McTavish said quietly, 'Your dinner's ready, if you want it.'

Kyle Lachlan swung on his heel, making the kilt flare, and strode to fling open the door to the dining room. Turning, he bowed low to Ilona, his face stony. 'Miss McGregor, if you please.'

Sooner than let him know how ashamed he had made her feel, Ilona straightened herself and stalked past him. Candles flickered on the great table and two places had been laid opposite each other. The light caught on crystal and silver, and glinted softly off the metal bosses of shields on the walls.

Before she could draw out a chair, Kyle Lachlan was beside her, doing the honours with old-fashioned courtesy so elaborate that she knew he was baiting her, but she thanked him coolly and sat down, occupying herself with unfolding the linen napkin while he strode round the table and seated himself.

Mrs McTavish served game soup and withdrew, leaving the two of them in lonely splendour.

'Do you always dine so formally?' Ilona asked when the fraught silence became unbearable.

'Not often,' he replied. 'But tonight we decided to do the thing properly, since we're honoured by the presence of a McGregor.'

She lifted her head, wanting to apologise, but the sight of him robbed her of words. The frills at his throat looked incredibly white, frothing on to the velvet jacket that shifted into different shades of green as the candlelight caught it, and against that white and green his hair was redder than ever, his skin deeply tanned. Handsome—no, not that, the word was too insipid for him. But attractive he certainly was, or would have been if his expression had been less forbidding.

Annoyed that her thoughts would not be kept in line, Ilona said stiffly, 'You can't really blame me for arriving as I did. There was no proper boat, and your letter wasn't very inviting. It gave me the impression you didn't want me here.'

'Perceptive of you.'

She stared at him in astonishment. 'You admit it?'

'Why should I lie about it?'

'You did lie! You said that Drumm was bleak and——'

'And so it can be!' he interrupted. 'How much of it have you seen? When the sun shines it's not so bad, but in the winter you wouldn't want to be here. Not when the wind blows and storms shake the foundations. Only the islanders like it—because it's their home—and more often than not the young ones leave as soon as they can. I only wished to save you the trouble and expense of a trip, but since you came anyway . . .' He waved a large brown hand, and shrugged. 'So be it. The choice was yours.'

'Quite,' said Ilona, applying herself to the tasty soup. She did not entirely accept his explanation, but at least she had tackled him about it and been granted some sort of answer.

The second course proved to be a roast, with vegetables cooked to perfection. While Mrs

McTavish served the food she did not once glance at Ilona. She was annoyed about being lied to, Ilona thought with a pang of conscience.

'What about yourself, Mr Lachlan?' she asked when the housekeeper had withdrawn again. 'Had you worked for my great-uncle for long?'

He glanced up, giving her a hard look. 'Long enough.'

'How long?'

No answer came. He went on eating his meal, ignoring her.

'I asked you . . .'

'I heard what you said. And I gave you my answer.'

'It was pretty unhelpful, though,' Ilona persisted. 'Long enough? Long enough for what?'

'Long enough to feel that I belong here, which is more than I can say for you, Miss McGregor. This island's no place for fluffy females. You have to be hardy to live here.'

'And what makes you think I'm not hardy?' she demanded.

His withering look, taking in her fragile appearance and light evening clothes, said it for him.

'Appearances can be deceptive,' she snapped.

'So they can, Miss McGregor. So they can. But we'll find out if you're as glasshouse-bred as you seem. Six months on Drumm will test your mettle.'

Ilona picked at her food disconsolately. He made island life sound grim. Was it really as bad as that, or was he exaggerating to worry her?

'You really didn't want me here, did you?' she said in a small voice.

'No, I did not.' His eyes met hers, flint-dark in the candlelight. 'But it was Hamish's wish.

Frankly, I didn't think you would want to come. I thought my offer would bring a welcome windfall.'

'Accepting did cross my mind,' Ilona admitted, 'but I was fascinated by the sound of the island. I had to see it. So I came.'

'Why?'

The single word hovered in the moving candlelight that struck red lights from his hair and turned hers to shining gold. Since she had not anticipated the question, Ilona had to search for an answer.

Eventually she let out a breathy laugh. 'Because I wanted to!'

'To see it?'

'Why, yes. How else could I decide whether I wanted it or not? Besides, I suppose I was bored and welcomed the thought of some excitement. Life in Surrey can be pretty deadly at times.'

His mouth twisted derisively. 'Poor little butterfly! Bored, were you? Well, I trust your taste for adventure has been dulled by yesterday's escapade. I don't want to have to rescue you from your own stupidity twice.'

Spots of angry colour burned on Ilona's cheekbones. 'Must you be so rude? It wasn't my fault.'

'That seems to be your theme song,' he said roughly. 'Don't you ever take the blame for your own actions? If you had written, I could have arranged for you to be met. Or you could have enquired about contacting me when you got to the coast. But honesty was the last thing on your mind, wasn't it? You were very careful to conceal your identity.'

She opened her mouth to protest, but clamped her lips shut again and pushed her plate away, telling herself there was no need to keep justifying herself like a guilty child.

'There were reasons for that,' she retorted, 'but since you're determined to think the worst I'll save my breath. You've got the wrong idea about me, Mr Lachlan. I'm not a delicate butterfly—I've had to work for my living. It isn't easy being brought up where you're not really wanted. Lately I've done nothing but skivvy for my aunt. Yes, I was ready for a change. Do you blame me?'

For a few moments he was silent, his gaze sliding over her with insolent intimacy to rest on the proud jut of young breasts beneath the fitted top of her dress. 'If you really expected me to be taken in by that sob-story,' he said at length, 'you should have dressed accordingly. You don't look the Cinderella type.'

Her flesh tingled under his scrutiny, but his words burned her pride. She had not intended to sound self-pitying.

'Or did you come down here looking like that to complete what you started this morning?' he growled.

Ilona did not at first understand what he meant, then a chill ran down her spine as she recalled how she had unwittingly displayed herself in Mrs McTavish's loose robe. Pushing back her chair, she stood up, her eyes darting green scorn. 'I don't have to stay and listen to your innuendoes!'

She started for the door, but before she reached it he had grasped her wrist, swinging her round, his free arm circling her waist with ease. Ilona struggled fiercely, battering at the white frills on his chest with as much success as if he had been a boulder. Shockingly, she felt herself drawn closer until the hard muscles of his thighs pressed against hers and she wondered suddenly—the thought made her head reel—just what he was wearing under that kilt!

'It's bad manners to walk out in the middle of a conversation,' he told her softly, his arm locked round her like a steel band.

Flinging her head back, Ilona stared up into the grim face with flashing grey eyes that told her he was not unaffected by his contact with her. What was it he had said about a shortage of women on the island? Surely he wouldn't——

'You can't force me to stay!' she cried. 'I shall leave as soon as the boat comes.'

His muscles tightened, flattening her against his body, and he lowered his face until it was only inches from hers. 'You forget that you belong to me, since I saved your life.'

'Let me go!' Ilona spat, terrified of his strength and the sheer male animal aura that encompassed her, threatening to overcome her utterly. 'You're nothing but a—a barbarian!'

She saw his eyes glitter, then he released her suddenly so that she stumbled back against the door.

'Barbarian, is it?' he said, very softly. 'You tempt me to prove it, but I very much doubt you'd be worth the trouble. Yes, run away—that's what I might have expected. You're a disgrace to the name of McGregor. Hamish asked for six months, but you'd turn tail after a day.'

'Maybe I don't want your island!' Ilona flared. 'Had that occurred to you?'

'You said you had to see it first. But go if you wish. Just remember, if you do leave, you'll inherit nothing. The moment you stepped on to Drumm my offer to buy became obsolete.'

Pale with shock, Ilona stared at him in dismay. 'You mean I've got to stay here for six full months, starting now, or . . .'

'Or you lose all claim to the estate,' he said with evident satisfaction. 'Now are you glad you came?'

Unable to stand his presence any longer, Ilona stalked out.

She paced the tower room, thinking furiously. For herself she didn't care if she gained nothing— her life would be no different from what it had been before she heard about the will. But Aunt Zoe would be furious. She had tried to persuade Ilona to accept Kyle Lachlan's offer. She had said Ilona would never stick to life on Drumm. Ilona had to prove that Aunt Zoe could be wrong.

Clearly Kyle Lachlan was being as unpleasant as he could in the hope of driving her away. He couldn't be allowed to win. Her great-uncle must have had some good reason for offering her a share of his property, and she couldn't let the old boy down by quitting before she had even begun. Let Kyle Lachlan do his worst—she was going to stay!

She slept restlessly, disturbed by the crying of the gulls, which never seemed to stop, but she must have been claimed by dreams at some point, because she woke to find that morning had come and Mrs McTavish was in the room, bringing her breakfast.

'I could have come down,' Ilona said feebly. 'There was no need to trouble yourself.'

'It's no trouble. I thought you'd be hungry. You barely touched your dinner, and you didn't stop for pudding.'

'No, I . . .' She bit her lip, troubled by the disapproving scowl on the housekeeper's face.

'Mrs McTavish, please forgive me for not being honest with you. I was afraid Mr Lachlan might be angry because I'd come unexpectedly, that's why I lied about my name, but I know it was wrong of me. And you've been so kind. Can't we be friends again?'

Throwing back the curtains to let the sun flood in, Mrs McTavish turned to look at the fragile girl, who was still pale after her ordeal in the sea. Poor lost child, the housekeeper thought, and her face softened as she came to tidy the bedcovers.

'I dare say we might be, dearie. No point in prolonging unpleasantness, is there? And you had cause to be fearful—he *was* angry.'

'Furious,' Ilona sighed. 'Oh, dear, I really didn't mean it to turn out this way. Is he always so hard to approach?'

Mrs McTavish folded her arms over her ample bosom. 'Aye, well, he does seem that way at times. But he hasn't had it easy. He misses the old man, and with Miss Morag not being here very often . . . I expect he gets lonely, like the rest of us.'

Lonely! Ilona could think of a lot more appropriate adjectives to apply to that unfeeling Gael. She had spent half the night listening for his footsteps, fearing that his 'loneliness' might get the better of him.

'Miss Morag is his . . .'

'His lady friend, Morag Frazer,' the housekeeper said at once, and laughed. 'I'd say his fiancée, but official engagements are out of style these days, aren't they? They've known each other a long time, but Miss Morag's had her career to think about. She's a journalist, you know.'

'Oh, is she?' Ilona remembered the photograph on Kyle's desk—the gorgeous brunette who had smiled so brilliantly for the cameraman. She had a feeling she would not like Morag Frazer.

'Anyway,' Mrs McTavish went on briskly, 'Mr Lachlan wants to know if you'd like him to show you the island. If you can be down in half an hour, he'll be waiting for you.'

Hurrying her breakfast, Ilona dashed down to the bathroom to shower, and dressed herself sensibly for island exploring, in jeans, thick sweater over a shirt, windcheater and flat-heeled walking shoes. She flicked a brush quickly through her hair and made for the hall, congratulating herself that she would not keep him waiting and give him an excuse to leave without her.

She fairly flew down the main stairs, arriving breathless and pink-cheeked, to have Kyle Lachlan look up from the chair where he sat reading a magazine and say with sarcasm, 'Where's the fire?'

'Mrs McTavish said half an hour,' Ilona gasped.

'Maybe she did, but not to a minute or two.' He rose to his full height, dressed in denims and the navy-blue sweater, his red hair combed into unruly waves. Sweeping a glance from her hair to her shoes, he lifted a sardonic eyebrow. 'Sure you can manage without your fur coat? The wind may be cold at this time of year.'

'What, one of your Atlantic gales?' she replied. 'I can take it if you can. It's really very kind of you to offer me a guided tour.'

'I was afraid you might go wandering off on your own if I didn't,' he returned. 'Then you'd probably have fallen off a cliff.'

'Wouldn't that have suited you?' Ilona asked archly.

His eyes returned her challenge levelly. 'Maybe. But I didn't fancy risking my neck to bring you

back. 'I've already had a ducking because of you.'
He bent to take a brown leather jacket from the
settee, shrugging his broad shoulders into it. 'Shall
we go?'

'I'm ready. How big is the island? Shall we need
the car?'

On his way to the main door, he paused and
looked back at her with a sharp laugh. 'Car? We
haven't even got a road. At times I use the Range
Rover, but usually on Drumm we walk.'

'Oh, good!' said Ilona, enjoying herself. 'I love
walking.'

Outside the main door the hill swept up and
round, with only a rough track running diagonally
across it. To the right the hill reached out to
shelter one side of the sea-loch, and below Creag
Mhor the gardens lay in terraces that stretched
down to the shore. A lone boulder, alive with
perching gulls, lay a few feet from the shore,
lapped round by water.

'Very bleak,' Ilona remarked as if to herself, her
eyes on a tree hung with yellow blossoms. 'Really
Drumm is quite barren, isn't it?'

From the corner of her eye she saw Kyle smile
grimly to himself. 'This part of it is sheltered. We
rarely have a frost—but then the Gulf Stream
warms the waters here. Even so, Hamish had to
take trouble to keep his gardens blooming the way
they do. They were his brain-child, his piece of
paradise—made by sweat and aching muscles out
of unhelpful land. But don't take my word for it—
come and see the rest.'

He strode off, long legs making light of the
climb up the track. Ilona hurried after him,
but as she approached the top the wind grew
fiercer, tossing her hair around her face, and she

felt the April chill in it.

'All right?' Kyle asked.

'I feel just fine,' she assured him, thinking that she would prove herself tough if it killed her.

He set off again, keeping to a slower pace that allowed her to stay beside him. One hand containing her flying hair, Ilona drank in the sight of moorland hilltops where the brown heather would soon be purpling to join the tender young bracken that grew in odd sheltered hollows. The island was really one big hill, full of gullies and small summits, with the highest point at the northern corner perhaps three miles away. Creag Mhor lay at the southern end of Drumm.

'What does it mean—Creag Mhor?' she asked.

'Big Crag. Not very exciting, is it?'

'It sounds better in Gaelic,' she laughed breathlessly. 'Oh——' They had topped a rise and the revealed view took her breath away. Before them lay the gentler slopes of the east side of the island, fields where cattle grazed lying beneath the brown tops where the sheep roamed, from where tracks converged on a small bay where the settlement lay. The houses were ranged round a harbour with a stone pier, where a few boats rested, but in all there were not more than twenty dwellings, she guessed.

'Not all the houses are occupied any more,' Kyle told her. 'I have a handful of men working on the land and there are a couple who catch lobsters, apart from the few old folk who've lived all their lives here. The women make knitwear—and there's a younger couple recently moved in. He writes and she does weaving.'

'I thought you didn't like strangers here,' commented Ilona.

The grey eyes were hard as granite. 'We don't. Mike Nevis—the writer—was born here and came back to escape the rat-race.'

She looked again at the view, spellbound. 'Well, whatever you say, it looks wonderful to me.'

'What you can't see from here are the cliffs,' he said with a wry smile that mocked her enchantment. 'To the north and west it's all cliffs. And that's it. Some hay for winter feed, some oats, a few vegetables the islanders grow in their gardens. Hard living, as I told you.'

'The living doesn't seem very hard at Creag Mhor,' Ilona said.

'No, but it's Hamish's private income that keeps the island alive. If it hadn't been for him, Drumm would be deserted now, like St Kilda and other places. As it is, most of the money goes on day-to-day expenses. Drumm can be a great responsibility, Miss McGregor.'

Irritated, because he seemed to be implying she was not equal to the challenge, Ilona queried, 'And you? What's your role?'

'I'm the factor. I see to the administration—the smooth running. Any problems end up on my desk to be solved. And at the moment I'm looking into the possibilities of expanding the arable land. I've had people out analysing the soil, but it's a complicated business. The land's deficient in certain essential elements, to begin with.'

Ilona frowned, a tendril of blonde hair wafting in front of her. 'I never was much good at science, I'm afraid.'

'Perhaps I can put it this way—farmers have a saying that goes: Under bracken gold, under gorse silver, under heather famine.' He swept an arm to encompass the heather-clad crags which made up

most of the island. 'As you can see, we shall none
of us get fat on what this land can produce
without help. But at least we'll try every avenue
before we admit defeat. Now let's go, before you
get blown to pieces.'

Realising that she had a great deal to learn if she
were seriously to consider accepting the inheritance, Ilona plodded after him on legs that soon
began to ache. She had underestimated the effects
of her brush with eternity, but she refused to admit
it in front of Kyle Lachlan.

It was about two miles further to the 'village',
but downhill most of the way. Kyle kept a pace
ahead, glancing back occasionally to see how she
was faring, and Ilona smiled brightly at him,
rewarded only by a bland, tell-nothing stare each
time. He was waiting for her to complain, but she
would not allow him the satisfaction.

As they reached the first of the houses, a woman
looked out of her door to greet Kyle in Gaelic and
stare curiously at Ilona. Gardens were neatly
tended, with flowers and bushes growing, and
windowboxes bright against polished panes.

Kyle pointed out one of the houses and
explained, 'That's Mrs McIver's. She keeps a small
store-room which isn't big enough to be a shop
but serves the same purpose. There's a radio-
phone there, too, and a private line for relaying
messages up to Creag Mhor. So in emergencies we
can be contacted. If ever you want to call home,
you can use the radio-phone.'

'All mod. cons, in fact,' Ilona said lightly.

At the next cottage an old woman dressed in
black sat knitting in her doorway. 'Fine morning,
Mr Lachlan,' she called.

'Yes, it is,' he replied. 'I've brought Miss

McGregor to look around.'

Her wrinkled old face showed no surprise; she only nodded and smiled, 'Good morning, Miss McGregor. I've got the kettle boiling if you'd care for a cup of tea.'

'Oh . . . yes, I'd love one if . . .' Ilona glanced uncertainly at Kyle, who said drily, 'Thirsty already? Well, take Mrs McVeigh up on the offer. I've got to see someone on business, which would probably bore you.'

Ilona pulled a face at his retreating back and opened the gate as her hostess rose from her stool, bidding her come into the cottage.

It proved to be a small two-room building, crammed with crude furniture and rather gloomy since it had only one small window. A kettle bubbled on a black-leaded hearth and in one corner stood a spinning wheel which was clearly not for decoration.

'Sit yourself down, lassie,' the old woman invited, straightening the black kerchief drawn round thin grey hair, and though her smile was warm her eyes shone with curiosity. 'You're feeling better now, I hope?'

'Much better, thank you.' Apparently everyone knew exactly what had happened to her. 'I'm really grateful for the rest, though. It's a stiff walk from Creag Mhor.'

'Well, at least you've got legs,' the old woman said mysteriously, pouring steaming water into a round brown pot.

'Legs?' Ilona queried. 'Oh, you mean I should be glad I wasn't seriously injured?'

The old woman grinned, showing gaps in her teeth. 'I mean you're human. Legs instead of a shiny, scaly tail. Not like the last mermaid who came here.'

Responding to the glint of mischief in the dark eyes, Ilona laughed. 'You're the third person who's mentioned her. Did she exist?'

'Of course she did!' Mrs McVeigh brought the pot to the table and sat down near Ilona. 'Your coming has brought it all back—the mermaid, and the Viking prince of Creag Mhor, and the dark-haired man from the sea, and poor Mairi. Shall I tell you the tale?'

'Please. I love legends.'

The old woman gave her a gratified look, said, 'You can call me Alice,' and poured two cups of strong tea. That duty done, she sat with a cup warming her hands and stared into the peat fire for what seemed a long time. Ilona waited, sensing the long-ago atmosphere of the cottage. She might have been a million miles from Surrey, in some other world.

'She was washed up on the shore of the loch,' the old woman began softly. 'Magnus Bright Axe, lord of Creag Mhor, found her there and fell in love with her, for she was beautiful. He took her to his castle and locked her away in the tower, fearing she might leave him.'

'And did she?' Ilona asked.

Alice Mcveigh glanced at her with faraway eyes. 'Listen and you'll hear . . . Oftentimes the mermaid would sit at her high window, looking down at the water and singing soft and sad, and from the sea there would come a dark-haired man who wandered the shore—a man who was not of the island.

'Then came the day that Magnus Bright Axe had to sail away to war. The mermaid's singing grew sadder. It could be heard all over the island. And the dark-haired man came more often to look up at the castle with longing.'

Something in the fire hissed briefly, making Ilona jump, but the old woman kept staring into space as if seeing visions, continuing in a mystic chant:

'There was a girl of the island called Mairi, who loved Magnus Bright Axe and desired to free him from the mermaid's spell. Although she was afraid of magic, she went down to the dark-haired man and offered her help in return for the granting of her dearest wish. He agreed to this, and Mairi unlocked the tower and set the mermaid free. She was heard singing for joy as she went down to join her lover on the shore.

'Mairi made her wish—a wish for Magnus Bright Axe to come home—to her and her alone— and the dark-haired man agreed it should be so. Then he turned into a black water-horse and rode off into the sea with the mermaid. Just at that moment, the ship of Magnus Bright Axe came round the point. He saw the mermaid leaving him and he leaped into the sea to stop her. But he was swept away.'

'How sad,' said Ilona.

The old woman threw up a blue-veined hand. 'Hush, there's more. Three days poor Mairi sat on a rock below the castle, weeping and praying to the water-spirit to grant her wish as he had promised, and eventually she was rewarded. Magnus Bright Axe came back—to her and her alone—for his dead body was washed up at her feet.'

In the silence that followed the tale's chilling end, Ilona could think of nothing to say. Alice McVeigh seemed lost in her trance, but she slowly returned to normal as she sipped her tea.

Drinking the strong brew as quickly as was

polite, Ilona took her leave, unsettled by the eerie
atmosphere that had pervaded the cottage while
the old woman recounted the legend in that
faraway voice. Mrs McVeigh accompanied her to
the gate, from where Ilona was irrationally
relieved to see Kyle striding up from the harbour.
At least he wasn't wearing that disturbing kilt,
though his jeans were almost like a second skin,
clinging to slim hips and long, muscular legs.

'And he, too, has Norse blood in his veins,'
Alice McVeigh said ominously before she padded
away and closed the door.

What could she mean? Ilona wondered, shivering
a little.

'Rested?' Kyle asked, head on one side
mockingly, his hair blown into wild red curls.
'What's wrong? She didn't slip a drop of the hard
stuff into your tea, did she?'

'No, I don't think so.' She glanced at the silent
cottage, wondering if the old woman could be a
witch; then she shook herself impatiently out of
the fey mood and added lightly, 'She told me the
legend. About Magnus Bright Axe and the
mermaid.'

'Well, you were bound to hear it sooner or later.
The whole island's waiting to see if history will
repeat itself.'

'How could it?' she asked, feeling tense for some
reason.

'It couldn't, even if it had really happened in the
first place. Alice McVeigh may swear that I have
Norse blood in my veins, but you, my dear Miss
McGregor, are demonstrably not a mermaid, not
with legs like yours. And there's no dark-haired
man pining for you, is there?'

Ilona sighed heavily. Oddly enough, she did

know a man with dark hair, but he was certainly not pining for her. He was off somewhere in the sun on an archaeological dig, hardly giving her a thought except to dash off a letter once in a while. There had been times when those letters had made her feel fizzy with excitement, but now she was only too sure that Hugh Danvers wrote to her out of habit.

'There you are, then,' said Kyle, taking her silence as agreement.

'I wouldn't be too sure of it, if I were you,' Ilona said crisply. 'As it happens, I do know someone who would fit the bill very nicely. Now all we need is someone to play poor Mairi.' She tilted her head to look at him directly, wondering if he might mention the beautiful brunette, Morag Frazer, his 'lady friend.'

'What, someone who's madly in love with me?' Kyle demanded, and threw back his lordly red head to shout with laughter. 'Oh, there are dozens of them. Dozens! I'm a great ladies' man, didn't you know?'

'You're modest, too,' Ilona said acidly.

CHAPTER FOUR

As if determined to test her mettle, Kyle set an impossible pace, heading for the centre of the island up a track that wound between meadows and climbed steeply to the moorland tops. Ilona, struggling behind, called out to him to stop, but was infuriated by the look of knowing satisfaction on his face as he strode back to where she stood with the wind whipping her hair behind her.

'Had enough?' he demanded.

'No, but your legs are longer than mine,' Ilona said crossly. 'And where are we going? Creag Mhor is over there.'

'I thought you wanted to see the island, so we're taking a detour. You might as well take a look at the wilder side, while we're about it. Or are you too tired?'

'I'm just fine, thank you!'

'Good. Then make your own pace. I'm used to striding out.'

Oh, damn the man! she thought bitterly, glaring at his departing back. He walked as though the going were paved and flat, but for her the ground seemed dangerously uneven, filled with humps and hollows, every downward slope leading to yet another climb. Still, she gamely trudged on across the heather, trying to ignore the nagging ache in her legs and the headache that was beginning to numb her brain, caused by the constant battering of the cold wind.

A group of sheep scattered as she approached

them, lambs tumbling after their mothers. Ilona's
eyes were drawn to the highest part of the island,
off to her right, which had a curious hump on top
accompanied by great weathered slabs of stone
standing erect. Perhaps it was an ancient burial
barrow, which would be interesting to explore, but
for now all her energy was engaged just following
Kyle.

He had stopped some way ahead, atop another
crest, and his voice came back on the wind, urging
her on before he disappeared again behind the
ridge of land.

'I'm coming!' Ilona yelled back, forcing her
protesting legs up the gentle incline as she
muttered imprecations under her breath.
Inhuman, that was another good word for that
great arrogant Scot.

Reaching the crest herself, she saw Kyle below,
standing right on the edge which dropped away
into nothingness. Birds screeched round the cliff,
wheeling in the air, and Ilona's mind spun with
them. Imagining that Kyle was falling, she flung a
hand to her mouth to cut off a cry as she thought
furiously that he was standing there deliberately,
just to frighten her. From below, waves thundered
against the cliff, foaming breakers rolling in from
the expanse of the Atlantic.

Not watching where she was going, she stepped
into a hole. Her ankle turned painfully and the
next thing she was falling, rolling helplessly, crying
out in alarm for fear of tumbling right off the cliff.
She was dizzily conscious of Kyle's tall figure
rushing out of the blue sky, then he was there,
holding her by the shoulders, looking anxiously
into her dazed face.

'Good grief, you're not fit to be let off the

leash!' he snarled at her. 'You have to watch your step up here.'

'I thought you were falling!' Ilona snapped back, disgusted to find she was on the verge of tears. 'Now I've twisted my ankle.'

'Which one?'

While she sat letting her breathing return to normal, he gently eased off her shoe and took her foot between hands that were surprisingly gentle, turning her ankle in a slow circle.

'At least it's not broken,' he said eventually. 'Do you think you can walk on it?'

She brushed at her face, trying to erase the shaming tears that stung her eyes. 'I'm sure I can, when I get my breath back. Oh—take your hands off me!' His touch made her flesh tingle and she was glad when he moved away to kneel on the grass beside her, the offending hands deep in his jacket pockets.

'So you're a McGregor after all,' he said. 'You're just as stubborn as Hamish was. Why didn't you say you were worn out?'

'I'm not.'

'You see? Stubborn as a mule. All right, we'll have a rest. You can occupy yourself contemplating the view.'

Only then did Ilona notice that the cliff was a bare two yards away. From where she sat she could see the rocks sweeping down into the sea, where a jumble of boulders glistened darkly before the next wave came and doused them in foam. The air was full of birds, screaming their annoyance at the two humans too close to their nests.

'There must be hundreds of them,' Ilona commented, retying her shoelace.

'Thousands.' Kyle twisted to look at the

whirling, noisy cloud. 'Gannets, guillemots ...
You wouldn't believe they were once in danger of
extinction here, would you?'

'Yes, I would. People used to catch them for
their oil and feathers.'

He looked back at her in surprise, the wind
making his hair toss round his craggy face. 'Who
told you that?'

'No one told me. I read up about the Western
Isles before I came, though there wasn't a lot
about Drumm itself.'

'It's pretty insignificant, compared to the main
islands.'

'Yes, I suppose so,' Ilona agreed, and stretched
out on her back, a hand across her eyes to guard
them from the sun. How exhausted she felt, and her
head hurt. 'Is it true that you have Viking ancestors?'

His voice came to her through the clamour of
seabirds and the pound of surf. 'It could be. The
Vikings got everywhere. Why?'

She shrugged. 'Just making conversation.'

'Thinking about the legend?' he asked in a
bantering tone.

'Maybe. Mrs McVeigh told it so mystically it
sent shivers down my spine.'

Rich laughter shook out of him. 'She's
renowned for that. She's a favourite at social
gatherings, when people fancy having their flesh
creep. But I would have thought you were much
too modern to be taken in by something like that.'

'I just thought it was sad,' Ilona said. 'Poor
Mairi, sitting on her rock for three days, only to
have her love turn up dead at her feet.'

She felt Kyle shift his position and when he
spoke his breath came warm on her cheek. 'Save
some sympathy for Magnus Bright Axe. He

drowned for love of a faithless mermaid.'

Something alerted her to the fact that they were very much alone on the cliff and she lifted her arm to see him bending over her. His eyes searched hers questioningly as he murmured, 'Do you fancy the idea of being a mermaid?'

Ilona sought for a coherent answer. Her heartbeat had quickened again, making her breathless as she stared up into the deeply-tanned face, into fathomless grey eyes that held her mesmerised. A nervous pulse beat in her throat, turning her voice into a croak.

'No, not particularly.'

As she tried to roll away his hands came on her shoulders, pinning her down among the heather, and he leaned closer, breathing, 'Wouldn't you like me to fall in love with you?'

'Will you please——' she began, but to her horror his lips stopped the words and he began to kiss her with slow sensuality. Ilona fought, but her hands only slid off his jacket and when she tried to kick he bent a knee across her legs, preventing her from moving. Her headache thudded spitefully, but as his mouth moved on hers she felt herself weakening. Something deep inside her bade her respond. The real world seemed to be fading, the sounds receding, and only Kyle was left, a warm weight half on top of her, his hands tangled now in her hair and his mouth hot, demanding that she obey that pagan urge.

Knowing that her arms were about to betray her and slide round him, Ilona twisted her head away and with a strength born of shame pushed at him in desperation. 'No! No!'

To her relief he moved at once, giving a wordless grunt of disgust, and Ilona sprang to her feet, wiping the back of her hand across her mouth as if she hoped to remove the imprint of his lips. She stood trembling, hardly believing that such horror had actually happened, and Kyle watched her with veiled eyes, his lips twisted.

'How dare you assault me like that?' she choked.

'Assault? I thought you were begging for it,' he said cynically. 'My mistake.'

'Oh, you——' Her vocabulary had no words to express her feelings. She turned and began to move away, only to find that her ankle was still sore. It caused her to limp, but she kept on up the slope, the wind chilling the tears that blinded her. She felt disgusted—with him and with herself.

She was not aware of his coming behind until she felt his hands on her, and as she turned to fend him off he bent and tossed her up into his arms, as easily as if she were a child.

'Put me down!' she cried.

'Oh, be quiet,' he growled. 'You can't walk properly. Stop being so stubborn. Just put your arms round my neck. It will make it easier for me. Do it!'

Ilona obeyed, furious with her own helplessness. 'I hate you!' she said with all the venom she could muster. 'You're nothing but a bully.'

'You're no angel yourself,' he returned. His profile was turned to her, his eyes narrowed against the sun and wind with tiny lines fanning out from them, and his mouth a taut line. 'But you needn't worry. Hamish guessed wrong, apparently.'

'I can't see what Uncle Hamish has to do with this,' Ilona said frostily, determined to keep him at a distance emotionally even though she was clasped tight against him, forced to sense every movement of his muscles as he strode along with her. His hair brushed her hands as she clasped them behind his neck, but she closed her mind against the softness of his red curls. His appeal was all to her senses, not to her heart, she told herself, and she had no intention of being misled by animal instincts—her own, or his.

'Hasn't it occurred to you that's maybe why he enticed you here?' asked Kyle. 'As a mate for me? Maybe to ensure that McGregor blood continues on this island?'

'That's ridiculous!' Ilona snapped.

He turned his head to look at her scathingly. 'I couldn't agree more, but I'll bet that's what Hamish had in mind.'

'Marry you?' she cried. 'You? If you were the last man on earth——'

'If I were the last man on earth,' he interrupted, 'there'd be plenty of others queueing up. You'd get trampled in the rush.'

'You have an exaggerated idea of your own charisma,' Ilona scoffed. 'Most women like their men at least half civilised.'

'And I,' he returned, 'like my women soft and tender. I hate to spoil your infantile imaginings, but cold, heartless mermaids are not to my taste.'

Ilona kept her thoughts to herself, only trying to impress her hatred on him by turning her face away and maintaining a chill silence. Cold, was she? Well, at least that meant he hadn't noticed how she had almost let his kisses overcome her better sense. Another few moments and she would have proved herself as warm as he desired.

When they reached the castle Mrs McTavish

came fussing round and insisted that Ilona should be put to bed at once. Kyle carried her up the stairs and laid her on the bed, leaving without a backward glance.

'Och, man, you're nothing but a fool at times!' Mrs McTavish chafed at him on the landing. 'Fancy dragging the lassie across the island so soon! She looks like death again. Give the girl time to get her strength back.'

Listening, Ilona, expected him to reply in angry terms, but he said nothing, and when the housekeeper came into the room it was apparent that Kyle had gone.

'Now, dearie, that's enough of this nonsense,' Mrs McTavish said briskly. 'If you're to stay, then you must take a few days to rest yourself properly. Don't worry about him—I'll see he keeps out of your way. He's just a daft, thoughtless man, that's all.'

Ilona was glad to obey. If she hadn't been goaded into action she might have realised she was still not strong. Now all she wanted to do was sleep. Resting would give her a respite from Kyle's presence, too.

Even so, she expected him to appear at any moment and was oddly disappointed when, every time the door opened, it was Mrs McTavish who appeared.

Two or three quiet days slipped by. Ilona occupied herself writing letters to friends and to her aunt and cousin, to tell them she would not be home yet.

To her surprise, the provision boat, when it came, brought a letter for her—from Hugh Danvers. 'The dark-haired man', Ilona thought, and wondered why a chill of apprehension ran through her.

'The laugh's on me,' Hugh wrote. 'I came home to see you and now it's you who have gone away. But what an incredible coincidence! You're on Drumm, and it so happens that I'm dying to take a look at the long barrow there. Tradition has it that it's a Viking burial place. May I come? If you say no I may turn up anyway. Do you still remember the night of the dance? I've thought about it often while I've been digging through oceans of sand. Please write straight away and tell me you remember, too. I've got a month's leave coming up. Love, Hugh.'

Smiling to herself, Ilona re-read the letter. Hugh's greatest passion had always been his work. But she did remember the dance. She had been eighteen, and thrilled by her first encounter with romance, but the next day Hugh had gone away and there had only been his occasional letters to fan flames which had turned to glowing embers and then to ashes. Yes, she remembered, but she was older now, a different person who knew that real love meant more than a few moonlight kisses. Still, it would be nice to see Hugh and have an ally.

She wrote inviting him to come and informing him of the days when the provision steamer would sail from the mainland; it would, if asked, bring a passenger, too.

'Mr Lachlan's gone to the mainland,' Mrs McTavish said one morning. 'He's spending the day with those soil experts of his, going over their reports, so you can get up if you feel well enough, and have the place to yourself.'

Thoroughly rested by her few days in bed, Ilona showered and dressed in casual clothes before setting about a proper exploration of the castle. Mrs McTavish joined her, retelling the history of various pieces of furniture and pictures. It seemed to Ilona that a good deal of money might be made by opening Creag Mhor to the public—though Kyle's red hair would probably turn white if she suggested it. He guarded his privacy fiercely.

Naturally she intended to tell him of Hugh Danvers's impending visit, for courtesy's sake, but she would certainly not ask his permission. She felt entitled, as her great-uncle's heir, to invite whomever she chose.

But why had Hamish McGregor included her in his will? Was it only in the hope of having her marry Kyle and produce half-McGregor children? She felt unsettled every time she thought of that, part of her recoiling in horror from the notion. But the rest of her—the part she couldn't control—kept dwelling on memory's of Kyle's warm strength, and once she had been shocked to wake and remember a dream of being wrapped fiercely in his arms, and enjoying it.

That evening as the sun set, Ilona sat reading by the fire in the great hall when she heard the helicopter come over the hill to settle on its landing pad on the shoulder of ground beside the castle. She looked up, listening as the sound faded into silence. Kyle had come home. Perhaps she ought to go to her room.

But why should she run away? She had her strength back now and Kyle's resentment might have cooled over the past few days. If she remained calm and aloof they might find some compromise that would enable them to live peacefully, if not amicably, while she remained on Drumm.

So she stayed by the fire, golden hair falling over one shoulder as she read her book, her shoes off and her feet tucked comfortably beneath her in the big chair. She wore a simple cotton skirt and shirt-blouse, with a cardigan for warmth, but then Kyle had accused her of tempting him when she dressed up, so the casual clothes would do very well for this meeting.

She heard the main door open but did not look up until a lilting female voice alerted her to the presence of a stranger.

'Darling, you've got to be joking!' the newcomer laughed as she stepped into the hall. 'I'm sure she isn't as bad as you make out. Surely you won't let a mere woman get on your nerves?'

'I may well throttle her before six months are out,' Kyle retorted.

Neither of them had noticed Ilona. Kyle was busy relieving the girl of her fake-fur jacket while she straightened her tight split skirt. Her dark hair was cut short in a sleek cap, with a winglike sweep falling over her eyes. From a distance she looked like a fashion model, a thin sweater clinging to almost boy-like curves and the slit skirt showing most of a slim leg.

This must be Morag Frazer, Ilona thought. Was that the sort of woman Kyle preferred? She looked hard as a diamond and her laugh sounded brittle. Yet Kyle was smiling at her in that faintly sardonic way he had, making Ilona's stomach give a curious quirk which she told herself was nausea.

Mincing on spindly heels, Morag approached the fire, pausing in surprise as she saw Ilona curled in the chair.

'Oh! Hello. You must be . . .'

'I'm the one he's going to throttle,' said Ilona, throwing a bleak glance at Kyle as he strolled after his girl-friend, hands thrust into the pockets of the tailored slacks he wore with a rollneck sweater. 'And you're Morag Frazer, I expect. How do you do.'

She climbed out of the chair, assuming an air of self-possession though she was acutely conscious of her stockinged feet. It was no help when Morag looked her up and down with open amusement, classing Ilona as no competition. The two shook hands briefly and Morag said, 'You're not at all what I expected. Kyle made you sound like a harridan.'

'You're not what I expected, either,' Ilona replied.

'Oh?' Morag preened herself, touching her hair and smoothing her sweater so that it showed the outline of bra-less breasts as she turned coquettishly to Kyle. 'What have you been saying about me, darling?'

'He hasn't even mentioned you,' said Ilona, wondering why she felt impelled to be waspish, except that she had disliked Morag on sight.

The dark girl batted luxuriant false eyelashes that framed her brown eyes with stiff spikes. 'I suppose Mrs McTavish has been gossiping again. Really, that woman ought to be reminded of her place! She behaves as though she's part of the family. Have a word with her, Kyle.'

'Mrs McTavish *is* part of the family,' Kyle said quietly, and folded himself into the chair opposite Ilona's, watching her with veiled eyes.

'Well, I certainly wouldn't let any employee of mine be so free with her venomous tongue,' Morag said coldly. 'Excuse me, I'm going to change for dinner.'

She stalked away, fetching an overnight bag from the entrance before climbing the stairs to one of the rooms off the gallery, obviously knowing exactly where she was going.

'Mrs McTavish keeps a bed made up in case of unexpected visitors,' Kyle answered Ilona's unspoken query, though she wondered why he felt obliged to explain. She was old enough to know that even if Morag did have a separate room there was every chance she wouldn't keep to it all night, not with a lusty man like Kyle around.

Irritated by the discomfort of that thought, she hovered uncertainly, wondering if she should escape to her room.

'How are you feeling now?' Kyle asked. 'Better for a few days' rest?'

'Quite my old self again, thank you. Do we always dress for dinner? Isn't that idea a bit dated?'

He shrugged, looking at the fire. 'Hamish liked a bit of formality when we had visitors.'

'Does Morag count as a visitor?'

He sent her an unreadable look. 'She does. But don't bother to doll yourself up for my benefit.'

Stung, Ilona resumed her chair. 'Then I'll save my energy. I'm sure I couldn't hope to compete with Morag, even if I wanted to. Perhaps I'll have dinner in my room and let the two of you have a cosy evening together.'

'You can do as you damn well please!' he exclaimed, coming out of the chair with a rush. 'Don't think it will bother me. *I* never wanted you here in the first place.'

Trembling from the fury in his voice, Ilona

watched as he strode across the hall and stamped up the stairs to his room, slamming the door with a bang that echoed round the panelled walls. What had she said to make him lose his temper so abruptly?

She was still tempted to retreat to her room, but curiosity held her where she was. Would Kyle put on his formal Highland dress for Morag's delectation?

No, when he eventually appeared he was wearing a charcoal-grey suit, and as he came down the stairs Ilona was pleased that he had not donned the kilt for Morag. He did look particularly splendid in that barbaric outfit, though now she came to think of it he looked good in almost anything—tousled in casual jeans, magnificent in tartan, or formal and elegant as he was now, the suit setting off his broad shoulders and long legs. She caught herself wondering what he looked like in bathing trunks, but was so appalled by the trend of her thoughts that she buried her head in the book to hide her burning face.

'Would you like a sherry?' he asked tonelessly.

'M'm? Oh—yes, please.' Covertly she watched as he opened a carved oak cupboard which held the drinks, her gaze wandering across his broad back, down the length of the tailored jacket and well-pressed trousers, and back again to the unruly red waves that shone in the light. Was Morag a regular visitor? she wondered. And was Kyle still angry? Perhaps she ought to use this opportunity to tell him about Hugh, but she didn't want to risk another outburst, not right then.

When he turned she averted her gaze so that he should not guess her thoughts as he strolled across to stand on the hearthrug, bringing her a full glass. She glanced up to thank him, but was silenced by the sombre look in his eyes.

'I'm glad you're feeling better,' he said in a low voice. 'It was my fault you were ill again. I'm sorry.'

Ilona couldn't have been more surprised, especially after the way he had stormed out only a short while before. 'You weren't entirely to blame. It was me—being stubborn, as you said.'

'Shall we call a truce, then?' he asked, slowly reaching a hand to touch her cheek with the lightest caress.

'If you like,' she replied, mystified by the change that had come over him. 'Kyle, are you all right?'

The hand whipped away from her as if she had bitten him. 'Do I have to be ill to be pleasant?'

'No! I didn't mean . . .' She started to get out of the chair, but the sherry spilled, wet drops plopping on to her skirt. Holding the dripping glass, she stood shaking out her skirt, embarrassed by her clumsiness, and just at that moment Morag carolled from the stairs, 'Here I am, darling. Sorry to keep you waiting.'

She was dressed in some silky material, all multi-coloured flounces about the long skirt, but the top hardly existed, and what there was of it was only just supported by shoestring straps. Ilona thought with chagrin that it was just as well she hadn't tried to compete. She didn't possess a dress that expensive, and anyway she couldn't have looked the way Morag did, so poised and stylishly thin. Suddenly she felt miserable.

Crossing the hall, Morag looked pointedly at the dark stains on Ilona's skirt. 'Oh, dear, have we had a little accident? Kyle darling, do get me a

drink—I'm parched! You'd better go and get
changed, Miss McGregor. I hope the stains will
wash out. It's a charming skirt, very girlish.'

Wanting only to escape, Ilona looked around
for somewhere to put her glass and found Kyle's
hand conveniently held out. She glanced up at
him, seeing sympathy in his eyes before she thrust
the glass at him and fled.

'I'll have dinner in my room,' she announced
from the stairs, keeping her back turned to the
pair below. 'Please ask Mrs McTavish if she
minds. I've got the most awful headache.'

In her room she sat on the bed breathing hard
and fighting tears, knowing she had made an utter
fool of herself. And Kyle . . . she couldn't forget
the way he had looked. Sorry for her! That was
unbearable. She could take his anger, but his pity
was too much.

She hardly touched her dinner, which caused
Mrs McTavish to tut worriedly. Ilona put herself
to bed straight afterwards and lay in the darkness
listening to the crying gulls and imagining Kyle
and Morag together by candlelight, or by firelight
in the great hall, or perhaps the more private
sitting room, or even in one of the bedrooms. Her
mind played vivid pictures, black hair tangled with
red, white limbs against a brown, muscular body.
But what did she care? She didn't care at all!

Morning found her more in control of herself and
she went down to breakfast in the sunny morning
room prepared to outface anything. The room was
empty, but Morag soon appeared wrapped in a
befrilled robe, her face already made up with the
false lashes fringing eyes that spat petulance.

'This place has gone downhill since Mr

McGregor died,' she said, helping herself to coffee.
'Creag Mhor used to be an oasis of gracious living
in this godforsaken wilderness, but now it appears
that good manners have gone with the wind. Mrs
McTavish tells me that Kyle has already break-
fasted and gone out.'

'I expect he had urgent business somewhere,'
said Ilona, cheered by the fact that Kyle hadn't
spent the night with Morag. Not the entire night,
anyway.

'So urgent that he couldn't wait to wish me
good morning? Oh, the sooner I get him away
from here the better.'

'Get him away?' Ilona queried, a sudden
stillness inside her. 'How do you mean? Doesn't he
intend to stay?'

Morag's sharp laugh cut across the room.
'Good heavens, you didn't expect him to spend the
rest of his life here, did you? He couldn't afford to
leave before. Positions as factor are hard to find,
even for a man of Kyle's capabilities. But now—at
least, when this ridiculous six-month thing is
settled—he'll have capital behind him. He can be
anything he chooses.'

'But he loves it here,' Ilona said incredulously.
'He's hoping to improve the land. That's a long-
term project.'

Lighting a cigarette, Morag blew smoke across
the table and smiled coldly. 'Of course it is, but if
he proves that it's possible the island will be that
much more attractive to a prospective buyer.'

Ilona felt as though she had been slapped. Kyle
was planning to sell Drumm, to walk out and
marry Morag? Was *that* why he had tried to buy
her off, why he didn't want her here—because he
didn't want to wait six months? Had he tried to get

rid of her so that he could sell the whole lot?

'But I thought ...' she faltered. 'He seems to care so much about the island, and the people. He enjoys helping them. He loves Drumm.'

A thin stream of smoke dribbled from Morag's nostrils. 'He's anxious not to let the place run to seed, naturally enough. It must be made viable, or no one will want to buy it. Do you think you know him better than I do? I assure you he will not stay here. No, before we're married he'll sell this miserable dump—or his half of it. You might start thinking how you're going to manage without him, Miss McGregor.'

CHAPTER FIVE

FEELING the need to get right away in order to think without interruption, Ilona asked Mrs McGregor to pack her a picnic lunch. She set off with the food and a tartan rug in a small rucksack slung over her shoulder, intent on exploring the island in her own time.

Crossing the shoulder of ground where a concrete pad had been built for the helicopter beside an old barn where the machine was kept, Ilona climbed up behind Creag Mhor. Overhead the gulls wheeled, as always, looking down at the slender figure with tossing golden hair as she set out for the north of the island, taking care to stay well away from the cultivated area. She walked slowly, so as not to tire herself too soon, pausing every now and then to examine a flower, but her thoughts were on Kyle. How totally she had misjudged him! He didn't care about the island, except for what he could gain from it. Poor Uncle Hamish, believing he had left the place in safe hands.

The heather passing underfoot reminded her of what had occurred on the cliff that day and despite herself she kept thinking about Kyle in a personal way, recalling how his body had felt against hers, and his mouth . . .

Eventually she found herself climbing the final slope to the summit of the island, where the standing stones pointed up to the sky like tapering fingers. She could see for miles on that clear day, out across the sea where lay more islands, some no bigger than 'boulders with waves constantly washing over them, and in the distance, like clouds on the horizon, lay the blue shapes of the mainland mountains.

Ilona sat down on the tartan rug, her back against one of the ancient stones as she opened her picnic boxes, discovering sandwiches, fruit, and a slab of rich shortbread, together with a flask of coffee. Before her the burial mound rose on the highest point on Drumm, a long barrow covered in tough grass, which took her mind to the legend. In his letter, Hugh Danvers had said the long barrow might be of Viking origin. Perhaps this was where Magnus Bright Axe had been buried, with solemn rites befitting a prince of the Norsemen, while poor Mairi wept her disillusion over the promises of water-spirits.

Morag, of course, could be cast as Mairi in the present drama, and if Hugh Danvers came to Drumm he would complete the quartet—the 'dark-haired man who was not of the island.' But he wouldn't be coming to claim Ilona, unfortunately. Nor was Kyle Lachlan likely to fall madly in love with her and drown himself if she left him. He wasn't the sort to care about anyone that deeply.

She shook herself, wondering why the silly legend persisted in haunting her. Coming to Drumm had seemed such an innocent escapade, but now she felt involved. She liked the island, liked its solitude and grandeur; she even liked those blessed gulls that were never silent for a minute. And as for Kyle . . . she despised his mercenary outlook, but there was no denying that she found him overpoweringly attractive physically, shaming though that was. It must be that

she had had so little experience of men. Aunt Zoe
had soon put paid to any incipient relationship,
but now Ilona found herself in close prosimity to a
devastating male animal, and the experience
unsettled her.

Until then she had not thought seriously about
staying on Drumm and actually claiming the
inheritance—after all, Great-uncle Hamish had
not owed her anything and she had expected
nothing from him. But now she felt that she alone
could protect Drumm from Kyle Lachlan's
planned desertion. Let him leave, if he wished;
there would be a McGregor to carry on the caring
tradition. Though she really couldn't imagine
Drumm without Kyle. The two were so right
together.

Hearing the helicopter clatter in the distance,
Ilona stood up, shading her eyes as the machine
swooped towards her, battering her with its wind
as it passed on its way to Creag Mhor. So Kyle
was back, but she was not yet ready to face him. If
he came looking for her she would be gone.

She packed away her picnic and moved on,
heading down the slope to the northern end of the
island. A path beckoned her feet to follow it, down
past rocky humps of land covered in heather and
short grass, to a spot from where she could see a
boulder-strewn cove below. The path led down,
taking a tortuous route across the hillside and
among the rocks, from where she saw a cave-
mouth gaping in the grey cliff that backed the
beach.

Birds came swooping round her, making her
throw up her hands. She was so occupied in
watching her step on the shifting rocks that she
failed to see the black clouds moving silently from

the ocean. The wind rose and the sunlight blinked out. Thunder rolled distantly.

Ilona glanced up as the first fat drops of rain spat down, leaving dark splotches on the boulders. To her horror, the rushing clouds appeared to be boiling inside themselves, turning daylight to dusk as they unfurled themselves across the sky, and out to sea a livid flare of lightning split the gloom. She would have to shelter in the cave.

The dark spots on the stones increased and joined as she stumbled across the jumbled boulders, the rain spitting cold on her scalp, damping her hair. With relief she gained the cave entrance and glanced behind as more thunder shook the world. The sea was slate-grey now, lifting itself to smash into the cove in foam-flecked waves, and the rain increased, slamming down like steel rods, the wind whipping it into the cave.

Shivering, Ilona retreated. After a few yards the tumble of rocks lessened, revealing the uneven floor of the cave. As her eyes became used to the half-light, she saw a natural buttress with a convenient boulder behind it, where she sat down huddled in her anorak, out of the worst of the cold draught.

The storm grew in intensity. Brilliant lightning lit the cave mouth like a stage and at the same moment a crack of thunder directly overhead seemed to shake the island. Ilona cowered, hugging herself for warmth, her eyes on the motionless rock around her as the thunder rolled away like a drummer at retreat. Kyle had said something about 'storms that shake the foundations,' she recalled. Well, she was experiencing that now, but it wasn't going to make her run away from Drumm.

She was miserably cold and damp, but there was no question of moving while the storm continued and the rain beat down like a waterfall across the cave-mouth. After a while the thunder moved away, but the rain didn't stop. It continued in a steady, soaking downpour which looked set to last for hours.

As the time passed she grew colder, and more afraid. Through the rain she could see that the tide was coming in, creeping up the beach towards her sanctuary. Suppose it covered the cave entrance! If only someone would come. But no one knew where she was. She had deliberately sought solitude.

Through the tumult of wind and rain she seemed to hear a voice. She strained her ears and the sound came again—someone calling her name. A tall figure appeared, dark against the cave-mouth, and Kyle's bass reverberated, 'Ilona!'

Thankful to see him, she stepped out from behind her protective buttress, but the next second recalled her doubts about him and the relieved smile vanished from her face.

'I'm here!'

She thought she heard him mutter, 'Thank God!' then he was making his way across the rocks behind the entrance. With some concern she saw that he was soaked through, wearing a sweater and jeans that clung to him wetly, his hair plastered to his head and water dripping down his face—a face that tautened with anger as he picked her out among the shadows.

'What the hell do you think you're playing at?' he said roughly. 'I've been combing the island for you.'

'There was no need to trouble yourself,' Ilona

replied in chill tones. 'I'm perfectly all right. I was just waiting for the rain to stop.'

Kyle swore softly under his breath. 'I didn't know that, did I? You've been gone for hours. You might have fallen off the cliff, or been lying with a broken leg on the moors, for all I knew. You're always doing something stupid!'

'Mrs McTavish knew I intended to be out all day!' she shot back. 'And if we're going to talk about stupidity, take a look at yourself—didn't you think to wear a coat?'

In the gloom, his grey eyes glowed murderously. 'I thought I had an oilskin in the Range Rover, but somebody's moved it. And then the blasted engine packed up on me. I've been hiking for miles.'

'Oh, really? Conscience troubling you, was it? I really don't need you to play nursemaid, you know.'

'No? Not when you fell in the sea? Not when you ricked your ankle? That's all the thanks I get for my trouble. You're nothing but a blasted nuisance, Ilona McGregor, and the sooner you get out of my hair the better for both of us!'

Fury ran hot through Ilona's veins, caused by her new-found protective instinct towards the island. 'You might as well know that I have no intention of leaving. I'm staying, whether you like it or not.'

He glared at her, seeming lost for an answer. 'Now I've probably caught my death of pneumonia, too,' he said at last. 'I suppose that would solve all your problems.'

While Ilona watched with growing amazement, he reached for the waist of his sweater and tugged the garment off, tossing it aside as he began to unbutton the wet shirt beneath. In the grey light his skin gleamed, muscles rippling across his smooth chest and shoulders, and for a moment Ilona feared he was going to remove his jeans, too, but with a bleak glance at her he moved away and began to gather all the dry material from the back of the cave—driftwood tossed up by the sea, grasses brought by birds, and even a cardboard carton left by some careless visitor.

Ilona resumed her seat on the boulder, watching as he gathered everything into a pile and reached in his jeans pocket for a battered matchbox. The box was damp, but eventually a match caught, a brilliant spark of light in the gloom, and as Kyle set it to the tinder the orange flicker glanced off the planes of his face and the hard curves of his torso. He looked more savage than ever, Ilona thought, but she must possess savage instincts herself because the sight of him stirred her oddly.

Slowly, the growing flames lit the cave, stirring in the wind that eddied round the walls. Kyle crouched by the fire, rubbing his arms and chest to dry them, little realising what he was doing to Ilona. Her fingers itched to touch that smooth, tanned skin and stroke the wet hair from his face, and her throat felt dry as she struggled with unfamiliar desires that dismayed her.

Remembering the tartan rug in her rucksack, she took it out and threw it down beside him, making him look round, at the tartan and then at her, his mouth grim.

'What's the matter? Does my nakedness offend you?'

'I thought——' she choked, cleared her throat and tried again, 'I thought it would keep you warmer.'

'How thoughtful,' he said with derision, but he slung the blanket round his shoulders and held his hands to the blaze.

Ilona got up and made her way round behind him to pick up his shirt, draping it across a rock where the heat could reach it. When she glanced at Kyle she found him watching her with twisted lips.

'Well, you've got to wear something when we get out of here!' she said crossly. 'I'm sorry if you object to my help.'

'It just seems out of character,' was his answer. 'So far you've done your best to louse up my life.'

'In what way?'

'Just by coming here!' He got to his feet, causing the blanket to slip from his shoulders. He caught it, looked once at Ilona and turned away, using the tartan to rough-dry his hair.

'I came here because my great-uncle seemed to want me to,' she told him tremulously. 'Your wishes didn't come into it. You were just his employee. Oh, I know you probably expected to be left the lot—you probably thought he was totally alone in the world and you could take advantage of him. But you were wrong. I'm learning a lot about you, Mr Kyle Lachlan. You're a vulture—a miserable, greedy——' She stopped as he swung round, raking a hand through his hair, his face so stormy that she stepped back, afraid that she had gone too far, especially when they were so alone. Hadn't she been warned that the Laird of Drumm would make her pay?

He took a step towards her and Ilona retreated. Her heel caught on something and she fell, knocking her elbow, but managed to scramble to her feet. She found herself against the wall of the cave, with nowhere else to go as Kyle's firelit shadow loomed over her, huge and grotesque, and Kyle himself approached with slow menace.

Her eyes widened as she flattened herself against the rock, wondering what he meant to do. 'Don't you dare touch me!' she gasped.

'Touch you?' he growled, and his hand shot out to fasten around her chin. 'But you're mine, little mermaid. Had you forgotten?'

As he bent over her, Ilona squirmed to be free, but his fingers held her jaw fast and the other hand slid round her waist, pulling her to him as he ground his mouth into hers. Her flailing hands slid across his bare ribs and pummelled the muscular back. But how cold he felt! And his jeans were clammy.

She had an insane urge to warm him. Her hands unclenched and lay flat against his back, her fingers rejoicing in the touch of firm flesh, and at the same moment his mouth became tender on hers, bringing a flush of fearful pleasure from deep inside her. Despite herself, she felt her lips parting beneath that sweet, determined assault and she swayed weakly against him, shuddering, while her fingernails drew patterns across his back.

He bent to kiss her throat, his lips finding the pulse that beat wildly there. Wanting him to stop, Ilona murmured his name but it came out soft and breathy like a sigh of pleasure. She was powerless to prevent the wave of longing that made her pliable in his hands.

Somehow he had unzipped her anorak and was lifting her sweater, his fingers lingering across the tender skin over her ribs, moving up to caress her breast through silky lace. Ilona heard herself moan as her body responded to the touch of his fingers as he teased and stroked, and it was as though her own voice woke her from heady dreams to stark reality. Guilt and shame swept through her and she grasped his wrist, trying to push his hand from her.

Kyle lifted his head. Eyes turned almost black by desire smouldered down into hers as he gently cupped her breast, muttering, 'What?'

'Stop it!' Ilona whispered desperately. 'Please!'

For a moment he hesitated, his gaze running over her face, lingering on full lips still swollen from his attentions. 'Why should I?'

'Because you're not really a barbarian,' she breathed, trembling. 'Unless you want me to hate you . . .'

Very slowly, he removed his hand from her and she tugged at her sweater, jerking away from him to fasten her anorak securely right up to the neck. She heard Kyle give a short, unpleasant laugh.

'Anybody would think you'd never been with a man before!'

Ilona looked round, her face flaming as she stared at him with huge green eyes. 'Is that so unbelievable?'

'Frankly, yes,' he said harshly. 'From the moment I first saw you—in that loose robe you used so effectively——'

'Oh, I hate you!' she flung at him, not knowing how else to defend herself.

'So you keep saying,' he snarled. 'And since you hate me whether I touch you or not I might as well . . .'

He made a move towards her and Ilona fled, stumbling over the uneven floor until she had put several yards between them. When she looked round he was still standing beyond the fire, the light flicking over his half-naked frame, making him look like a Red Indian brave, and his mouth was curved in mocking humour.

'Calm yourself,' he said, throwing out a disinterested hand. 'The mood's gone. Besides, I never yet forced a woman. Why should I break the habit of a lifetime for a frigid little wench like you? There are plenty of other women.'

'On this island? Oh, but of course Morag's here at the moment, isn't she?'

Languidly, he bent and picked up the tartan, throwing it round his bare shoulders. 'No, she left this morning. I flew her back to the mainland.'

'And as soon as she was out of reach you came after me? How would she feel if she knew what you just tried to do?'

In the firelight his face was an enigmatic mask, unfeeling as a carving on a totem pole. 'I haven't the slightest idea.'

'You're despicable!' Ilona spat.

'I'm myself—Kyle Lachlan, Laird of Drumm.'

'Oh, yes! Until you sell it.'

A deep frown furrowed his brow. 'Sell it?'

'Morag told me about your plans. That's why you didn't want me here, isn't it? You wanted everything in your name alone, so that you could dispose of it to the highest bidder.'

He was silent for a while, watching her. 'And if I did, what do you plan to do about it?'

'I'll fight you!' she said fiercely. 'I'll fight you with all the means at my disposal, to protect my great-uncle's memory. Drumm shall not be sold to someone who doesn't care about it!'

She faced him defiantly, her head high. What she expected him to do she wasn't sure, but it certainly wasn't what he actually did—which was burst into laughter, rich and rumbling, echoing round the cave.

Disconcerted, Ilona turned away. He was a strange puzzle, a man of lightning moods as changeable as the seas that washed his island. She didn't understand him at all.

As she moved restlessly towards the mouth of the cave she realised that the rain had stopped. A low shaft of sunlight speared in, glinting across the wet rocks, and when Ilona clambered to the entrance she saw the sun peering beneath the clouds, lighting their undersides to pink and gold, and flaming on the surface of the ocean. It was a beautiful sight she was to remember for a long time, an omen which told her she had chosen the right pathway. Drumm welcomed her, even if its master did not.

To judge from Kyle's behaviour, one would have thought that nothing unusual had passed between them. He shrugged into his half-dry shirt, picked up his soaking sweater and her rucksack, and came to the cave entrance to join her.

'It's turned into a pleasant evening,' he remarked.

'Yes.' She couldn't bear to look at him. She was full of shame for what had occurred in the cave and her skin still trembled every time she thought of his hands on her. How could she have forgotten all the years of training in Aunt Zoe's puritan household? It was Kyle's fault. He was such an arrogant brute he thought no woman could resist him.

But her honest nature reminded her that she had not been blameless. Her resistance had been lukewarm even before it melted altogether. Why did Kyle have such an effect on her?

She glanced up at his profile, her eyes troubled, and he turned his head to give her a smile full of immense charm and just a little teasing, so that Ilona felt flustered and moved away. Would she ever comprehend what went on inside that red head of his?

After that, her life on Drumm assumed a comfortable routine and her relationship with Kyle, if not friendly, was at least not fraught with the sort of tensions she had come to expect. She seldom saw him except at dinner, when he spoke of his work about the island, the people he met, and incidents that had either amused or annoyed him. But there were occasions when he didn't turn up for the evening meal and Mrs McTavish said he had had to go to Skye, or Uist, or one of the other islands. Visiting girl-friends? Ilona wondered, but she didn't ask for fear her interest in Kyle's movements aroused the housekeeper's suspicions.

Three full weeks slipped by.

A period of wet weather was followed by days of mist when Ilona didn't venture far from Creag Mhor, but when the sun reappeared it was noticeably warmer and she was surprised to realise that May had almost ended. At this rate the six months trial period would soon pass.

But she didn't believe the same even tenor of life would continue for that length of time. She was aware of a feeling of expectancy, as when the earth grows still before a storm. Although Kyle kept his distance and was polite to her there were times when she caught him watching her with an odd expression she could not interpret, and for her part she was increasingly aware of him. If she heard the helicopter land, or when the sun was going down, her stomach knotted itself in anticipation of meeting Kyle. Sometimes, if he happened to pass near her, her body stiffened in expectation of contact with him—wanting it and yet not wanting it. She understood neither herself nor him.

She passed her time with Mrs McTavish, listening to tales of her great-uncle and the history of the island, or sat reading from weighty tomes in an effort to educate herself for her new role. Talking with Kyle helped, too, for he told her about the problems and small triumphs which gave colour to island life. His attitude puzzled Ilona; if he didn't care about Drumm then he was a brilliant actor. But perhaps he was thinking more of Morag by planning to sell his share, since the dark girl had made it clear she would never live on the island.

On an afternoon much like any other, when Ilona was busy polishing the banisters, she was astounded to hear someone hammer on the great doorknocker at the main door. How very odd! No one ever knocked at that door. If the islanders called it was always at the rear entrance.

Laying her duster aside, she went to open the door and gaped in disbelief at the dark-haired man who smiled at her—her archaeologist friend, Hugh Danvers.

'Hello, Ilona,' he said cheerfully. 'I was going to write and warn you, but then I decided to give you a surprise. I came over on the steamer. Well, aren't you going to invite me in?'

Regaining her composure, Ilona opened the door wider. 'Of course. I was just . . . It certainly is a surprise!'

More than he knew, for she had not told Kyle Hugh might be coming. She had intended to, but the moment had never seemed right and she had been waiting for Hugh to inform her of the date of his arrival.

Hugh picked up the suitcase he had left on the ground and stepped inside the hall, looking round at the homely opulence of the place. 'Very nice. *Very* nice.'

'Yes, we think so, but ... Oh, Hugh, I do wish you'd warned me you were coming.'

His gaze sharpened on her face. 'Why? What is all this, anyway? When I asked for passage aboard the steamer I got some very funny looks, and when I came through the village the people stared at me as if I were a little green man from Mars.'

'It's just that ... they're not used to strangers. We don't get many outsiders on Drumm. And I'm afraid I haven't told Kyle you were coming.'

'Kyle? Oh, your estate manager? It's none of his business, surely? Anyway, I'm here, even though the islanders seemed reluctant to tell me where to come. It's good to see you, Ilona. You look as if life here suits you.'

Something in his eyes told her he was thinking about kissing her, so she moved away swiftly. 'I'll show you your room. I expect you could do with a cup of tea after your journey.'

Having shown Hugh the guest room, she went down to ask Mrs McTavish to make some tea. The housekeeper was surprised to learn that they had a visitor, but Ilona didn't linger to be told what she already knew—that Kyle wasn't going to be pleased.

She and Hugh were in the hall, taking tea in front of a fire recently lit in anticipation of the evening chill, when to her horror Kyle walked in. Ilona had not expected him yet, had wanted to explain to him before he met Hugh, but here he was, striding in, stopping dead as he registered the cosily domestic scene at his own hearth.

Seeing his face tighten, Ilona leapt to her feet, berating herself for forgetting the jungle telegraph that worked like magic on the island. Someone had obviously told Kyle about the arrival of a stranger who had asked the way to Creag Mhor.

'Oh, Kyle,' she said with an uncertain smile. 'This is Hugh Danvers, a friend of mine. He came over on the boat and I've invited him to stay for a few days.'

Kyle's eyes slid to Hugh, who was also on his feet, and snapped back to glare at Ilona with all the warmth of an Arctic winter. 'Without even a word to me?'

'Well, I wasn't sure exactly when . . .'

'Miss McGregor surely doesn't need your permission to invite her friends to her own house?' Hugh put in.

'*Her* house?' Kyle growled.

'Half mine,' Ilona said quickly, wishing he wouldn't glower so. Her nerves all stood to attention when he looked that way. 'I did invite Hugh to come, but I didn't know when he'd be arriving or I would have told you . . .' The words trailed off feebly as his expression darkened even further.

'This house is not half yours,' he reminded her in a low voice full of fury. 'Not for another five months, it isn't. It's *my* home, and I won't have strangers coming uninvited. Strangers are not welcome on Drumm.'

'He's not a stranger—not to me,' Ilona argued.

The look Kyle flung at Hugh was eloquent with insults. 'I'm sure he's not. But he's still not welcome, as he knows very well if he's the Hugh

Danvers I'm thinking of. Something to do with archaeology?'

Ilona felt confused. How did he know about Hugh's profession? But Hugh was saying smoothly, 'Yes, that's right. You have a good memory, Mr Lachlan. I did write several times to Mr McGregor asking for his permission to excavate the long barrow and . . .'

'And you were told,' Kyle said evenly, 'to stay away from Drumm. The long barrow is not to be disturbed—not under any circumstances.'

'Oh, come' Hugh replied with a laugh. 'What harm will it do? It might bring a few tourists, who'd be only too ready to spend their money. You could sell your island knitwear, and open a café, maybe even a small hotel.'

'Tourists?' Kyle spat the word as if it tasted vile. 'You've had a wasted journey, Mr Danvers. There's nothing here for you. And if you attempt to disturb the barrow, I warn you—you'll have to go through me to do it!'

CHAPTER SIX

TROUBLED by the memory of that scene in the hall, Ilona decided to present a picture of fragile femininity that evening, in the hope of averting Kyle's temper. She had packed one long evening dress, though she had not yet worn it, and hadn't Kyle said that formality was called for when visitors were present? He would probably wear the kilt, to establish himself as master of Creag Mhor for Hugh's benefit.

The dress was shell-pink, covered in a layer of matching chiffon, fitting closely except where it flared from the knees. Cape sleeves had been cut to form part of the bodice, which was scooped deeply at the front, and to complement it Ilona pinned her hair into a shining coronet with a few softening ends left free. Regarding her reflection in the mirror as she fastened a silver necklet, she mused that Kyle couldn't possibly be angry with her when she looked that way, especially if she was sweet and winning with him—except that she was depressingly certain that Kyle's temper, once roused, would not be stilled by any woman's charms.

As she went down the stairs, Mrs McTavish was crossing the hall, but looked up and smiled at the sight Ilona made.

'Och, you look beautiful!' she declared. 'He must be special, eh?'

'Special?' Ilona said blankly.

'Your young man. He's very good-looking, isn't he?'

'Oh . . . you mean Hugh? Yes, I suppose he is.' She meant that he was good-looking, but Mrs McTavish misunderstood and answered knowingly.

'Aye, I thought so. Well, you'll have him all to yourself tonight.'

She would have gone on her way, but Ilona queried, 'Isn't Kyle having dinner with us?'

'Why, no, dearie. Did you not hear the helicopter go off? He's gone to the mainland. Got a date with Miss Morag, so he said. Both of you'll be having a fine time tonight.'

Something twisted in Ilona's stomach. Gone to meet Morag? When she had dressed up especially and was hoping to see him in full finery, if only to prove to Hugh that Kyle was something more than just the estate manager? Oh, no!

But there was no time to wonder at her own feelings of disappointment, for here came Hugh, wearing a lounge suit, smiling and telling her she looked wonderful.

'Honestly, Ilona,' he said as they dined. 'I must say I don't think much to Lachlan's attitude. I realise that, officially, you have to live here for a while before you can say it's yours, but it was a bit thick when he tore into me that way. What's he got against tourists?'

'He says too many visitors would trample the crops, frighten the sheep, alarm the bird colonies, and drop litter,' she replied, toying with her food, still feeling strangely lost without Kyle. Where was he now? What were he and Morag doing? 'Besides, the islanders are private people. They'd feel as if they were in a zoo. It isn't only Kyle who doesn't like the idea of tourists. And if people did come, what is there for them to do here?'

'Get a breath of real fresh air, and see unspoiled countryside.'

'They can do that on the mainland. Drumm's so small it wouldn't stay unspoiled for long. And if people want to visit islands there's Skye and Lewis and all the rest, which are big enough to cope. There's nothing special on Drumm.'

'There's the long barrow.'

'That's not unique to Drumm,' she said with a sigh, wishing the main lights were on. Mrs McTavish had thoughtfully lit the candles, but it seemed a pointless display when the man opposite her had plain dark hair, not red that glinted flame when the light caught it. 'And, Hugh, you didn't tell me you'd written to my great-uncle and been refused permission to look at the long barrow.'

He couldn't meet her eyes. 'I didn't want you to think that was my only reason for coming. It's true that I would love to excavate it, but I wanted to spend some time with you, too. And,' he lifted soulful brown eyes, 'you're worth looking at, Ilona. I've missed you. Do you ever think about that time in Surrey? You were like a flower, just opening for the first time. And now you're in full bloom.'

'Thank you,' said Ilona, only half listening. Events of three years ago seemed irrelevant, as if they had happened to someone else. Hugh hadn't changed, but somehow his deep brown eyes and classic features seemed less attractive than they had been before, and she was fairly sure, whatever he said, that the barrow had provided a bigger lure to him than the chance of her company.

He began to tell her about his excavations in Egypt, where he had been engaged on a dig, and

though she listened and made appropriate replies
she couldn't feel real interest in what he was
saying. Kyle had stalked out of the hall earlier on,
but she knew he wouldn't just stand by and let
Hugh carry on. That wasn't Kyle's way at all.

But then she hadn't thought he would disappear
for the evening, leaving her alone with Hugh.
Wasn't he just the tiniest bit jealous? But why
should he be? He had told her often enough that
he wasn't interested in her personally, and his
polite distance during the past weeks seemed to
confirm it.

After dinner she and Hugh sat by the fire
finishing the wine, which made Ilona sleepy.
Several times she found herself having to
concentrate hard to follow what Hugh was saying,
and all the time she was thinking about Kyle—so
much so that she thought she heard the helicopter
return, but it could only be the wind around the
castle. Kyle wouldn't be home for hours, if at all
that night. The thought made her so miserable she
could have burst into tears.

'You're tired, aren't you?' said Hugh. 'Or am I
being boring? Shall we go to bed?'

Instantly she was wide awake, ready to fend him
off as he rose from his chair and came towards
her.

'I meant,' Hugh explained with a laugh,
'separately. Good heavens, what do you take me
for? Anyway, you're almost asleep.' He bent over,
hands braced on the padded arms of her chair, and
dropped a light kiss on her forehead before smiling
into her eyes. 'It's really good to be with you,
Ilona. I've missed you.'

'I've ... missed you, too,' she replied, not
entirely truthfully, but he was nice and she

didn't want to hurt him.

Neither of them realised that Kyle had come in silently until his sardonic voice made Hugh straighten as if he had been stung.

'Am I interrupting something?'

'We were . . .' Hugh hesitated, 'just saying goodnight. If you'll excuse me, I'll get to bed. It's been a long day, travelling and one thing and another. Goodnight, Lachlan.'

Kyle did not deign to reply. He stood unmoving, hands thrust deep into the trouser pockets of his suit, as Hugh passed him and made for the stairs.

'You're home early,' remarked Ilona, sliding out of her chair.

'Too early, by the looks of things. I do apologise.'

She smoothed down her dress, giving him a venomous glance. 'There's no need to be crude. How's Morag?'

'Fine, thank you.'

'Would you like a drink?' she asked, but as she moved she felt unsteady and Kyle strode to her side, grasping her wrist. When she looked up at him she saw that he was angry, his eyes darting grey ice-crystals at her.

'Got you drunk, has he?' he demanded.

'No, certainly not! Mrs McTavish put out a bottle of wine and it seems to have gone to my head a little.'

'That and the scintillating company of Mr Danvers, no doubt.'

Ilona tilted her chin, glaring mutinously up at him. 'Is that any business of yours?'

His gaze slid down her white throat to the soft swell of flesh visible beneath her dress. She heard his breathing quicken and the fingers around her wrist tightened.

'When you've quite finished ogling!' she muttered, and jerked free of him, rubbing her wrist. 'That's one thing I didn't have to put up with from Hugh.'

'No?' he growled. 'Didn't he appreciate the trouble you'd gone to to make yourself alluring for him? How disappointing for you! But perhaps he's not man enough to respond to such an open invitation.'

'He's not like you, if that's what you mean,' she shot back. 'There must be something wrong with you if you can come straight from Morag and still feel the need to prove your masculinity. Some men have more self-control, thank heaven.'

'Self-control?' he got out under his breath. 'My God, Ilona . . .' With an impatient movement he swung away, thrusting a hand into his hair as he leaned on the mantel above the fire. 'Go to bed, will you? And you can tell your Mr Danvers that I expect him to leave in the morning. I'll take him to the mainland in the chopper.'

'You will not! Hugh's staying for a few days, as *my* guest.'

Kyle swung back to glare at her, saying through his teeth, 'Not in *my* house, he isn't. He goes first thing in the morning, or I swear I shall personally throw him off this island and let him swim for it!'

She did not fully understand why he was so determined to get rid of Hugh. For a few seconds she returned his angry look with green fire of her own before saying flatly, 'I'm sick and tired of hearing you lay sole claim to everything, Kyle. My great-uncle left his estate between us—jointly. I have as many rights here as you do, and you'd better get used to the idea. And while we're on the subject, hadn't we better start sorting out the financial side? Who's paying the bills, for a start?'

'The solicitors are handling everything. Nothing can be finalised until the six months are over.'

'I see. Well, as long as we have things clear, I'll say goodnight.'

As she reached the gallery she thought she heard him say, 'Goodnight,' but when she glanced round he had his back to her, his red head bent towards the flames as if he were weary.

Of course he would be weary after an evening spent with Morag, she thought venomously. But why did the thought of Kyle with Morag disturb her so?

In the morning when Ilona went down to breakfast Mrs McTavish told her that Kyle had gone about his work, but he had promised to be on hand at ten o'clock to take Hugh to the mainland. Furious that he still wanted Hugh to leave, Ilona poured herself a coffee and buttered some toast, waiting for Hugh to join her.

'He said he'd throw me off the island?' he enquired incredulously when she told him of her altercation with Kyle. 'He can't do that!'

'He's quite capable of it,' Ilona replied. 'Look, Hugh, sooner than have more arguments, will you go with him and wait somewhere until I have a chance to reason with him? There's a nice little inn where you could stay quite cheaply.'

'For how long?' Hugh demanded.

'I'm not sure, but I'll soon know if he's really determined not to have the barrow disturbed. If I can't move him, you might as well forget about it.'

Hugh gave an exasperated groan. 'But I've come

all this way! Aren't I even to see it? I brought a
camera to take photographs—I was going to do
some measuring. There's a lot of preliminary stuff
wants doing before we actually break soil. Darn it,
Ilona, nobody's ever had a really good look at that
long barrow and here I am not—what, three
miles?—away from it. Don't you understand how
frustrating that is?'

She stirred a second cup of coffee, frowning.
Just to let Hugh look at the place couldn't do any
harm, surely? 'Perhaps if we hurry ... Kyle
certainly won't leave without you.'

'Bless you!' smiled Hugh. 'I'll go and get my
camera.'

The ubiquitous gulls wheeled on currents of warm
air over the long barrow and the morning sun sent
long shadows from the base of the guardian
megaliths. Glad to rest after the hurried walk they
had taken, Ilona leaned against one of the stones
while Hugh studied the barrow from all angles,
exclaiming over its archaeological possibilities.
After a while he took out his camera and began to
take pictures.

'Smile!' he ordered with a laugh, coming
opposite Ilona. 'Good, that's one for my wallet.
You know, Lachlan has no right to be so dog-in-
the-manger. The long barrow belongs to history,
not to him.'

'He just hates the thought of anything disturbing
the island,' Ilona explained.

He looked at her sharply. 'You sound as though
you're inclined to agree with him. Has he
brainwashed you?'

'No, of course not.'

Leaving his preoccupation with the barrow,

Hugh came to stand beside her. 'You're still my girl, Ilona.'

'Was I ever your girl?' she asked sadly. 'That isn't the way I remember it.'

'But you were very young. I didn't want to get too serious when I knew I wouldn't be staying in Surrey, but now . . .'

Before she could prevent him, he had thrown his arms around her and was kissing her. Ilona stiffened, about to push him away, but a hand on Hugh's shoulder jerked him round to stare at Kyle, who stood glaring at the other man with black fury.

'I told you to keep away from here! I've brought the Range Rover to take you back to Creag Mhor. It's down that track, waiting for you. Are you going, or do I have to force you?'

Red-faced, Hugh rubbed the shoulder which Kyle had used so violently. 'The law might have something to say about that. All right, I'm coming. Ilona, you know where you can reach me.'

'Wait!' Kyle wrenched the camera from his hand, opened it with one deft flick of his fingers and let the film flip out into the light, ruining it.

'Kyle!' Ilona gasped, but he silenced her with one livid look and took from his pocket a five-pound note which he stuffed into the camera before handing it back to Hugh, who looked as if lightning had struck him.

'That will buy you another film,' Kyle growled. 'Now get back to the Range Rover before I do something we shall both be sorry for!'

Hugh glanced at the camera, at Ilona, at Kyle, and thought better of arguing. Squaring his

shoulders, he set off along the track which wound
out of sight behind a shoulder of hillside.

The standing stone felt hard to Ilona's back as
she pressed herself against it, wondering what Kyle
intended to do with her now that Hugh had gone
from sight. He stood frowning into the distance,
eyes narrowed against the sunlight, his lips pressed
so tightly together they were rimmed with white.

Unable to bear the tension, Ilona said in a low
voice, 'You really are a bully, aren't you? What
harm was he doing?'

'You deliberately defied me,' he replied, spitting
her with a look of cold rage. 'Can you really see us
acting as business partners? Hamish must have
been mad. I know what I'm doing, but you ...
Everything you do is calculated to go against me.'

That wasn't true, she thought, but she couldn't
put her mind to an appropriate answer, not when
he stood a bare two feet away. If he reached for
her she would fight him off. But in an odd,
masochistic way, she wanted him to reach out, to
break the physical tension which had been growing
in her for weeks.

'I still don't see what harm he was doing,' she
protested.

'No, you wouldn't. And I don't feel inclined to
explain myself—especially not to a spoilt, wilful
child like you.'

'I'm not a child!' Ilona gasped.

'Then stop behaving like one or I'll ...' He
reached out a hand and she caught her breath,
flattening herself against the stone, her eyes huge
and green in a face gone suddenly pale.

With a muttered exclamation, Kyle let his hand
drop without touching her. 'Do you want a lift
back?'

'I'd prefer to walk!' she spat.

'Suit yourself.' Shrugging, he swung away to stride in Hugh's wake, leaving Ilona shaking with reaction. Thank heaven he hadn't touched her! But oh, she had wanted him to touch her, had wanted things she couldn't put a name to. Her lips, of their own accord, seemed to ache for the touch of his firm mouth and she laid her fingers on them, wondering at the treachery of her own senses.

As she returned to Creag Mhor the helicopter took off, heading for the mainland with Hugh aboard, and clouds began to pile up from the west, turning the air cold as the breeze freshened. Soon after Ilona gained the shelter of the castle a soft drizzle started, misting the distances.

Feeling bored and restless, she took herself into the study where Kyle spent hours of his working day, intending to find a book on sheep-rearing. But as she took down the book and went to sit at the desk she saw a file left there, headed 'Reports.' Although she had never been much good on scientific matters, she laid aside her book and began to flip through the file.

She discovered a bewildering mass of typed pages, written in stilted, formal English that made her brain ache as she tried to follow the mysterious references to soil composition, mica and kaolin, calcium carbonate deficiency, protozoa, and something called 'podzols.' It might have been written in Greek for all the sense she could make of it.

Then a phrase leapt up at her from one of the pages—'oil-bearing deposits.' Oil? Was there oil on Drumm? Surely——

At that moment Mrs McTavish appeared, coming to vacuum the study. Ilona slapped the file shut with a feeling of guilt, picked up the book on sheep and left the housekeeper to do her work in peace. But even though she sat by the fire with the heavy farming book open on her lap her mind was on that report. She felt nearly sick with disgust and misery when she thought of it. Oil! So that was Kyle's secret. No wonder he didn't want her poking about in his study!

Of course he hadn't wanted her to come, and now didn't want her to stay. He was afraid she might discover that Drumm was the source of the 'black gold' that could bring riches!

When the housekeeper had finished in the study, Ilona returned to the desk with the idea of reading the report in detail. But the desk was bare—even Morag's photograph had gone—and search as she would she could not find that file anywhere. She almost went to ask Mrs McTavish what she had done with it, but the housekeeper would only have told Kyle. He mustn't guess that she now knew exactly what he was up to.

After lunch, wearing her hooded blue raincoat, Ilona set out to walk down to the settlement. The rain drifted like mist across the hills and sea, only enhancing the lonely beauty of the place. Imagining it devastated by oil wells, huge lorries and ugly gashes across the land, Ilona fumed against Kyle Lachlan. It wasn't as if they really needed the money—well, she didn't, though Morag probably wouldn't refuse an extra million or two. But it would be desecration! She would not let him do it. He had accused her of defying him and now she was going to live up to that slur, because Kyle didn't really care about Drumm. But she did! She was going to establish her rights once and for all.

One or two people waved to her from cottage

windows as she walked down the single street and
called at Mrs McIver's to ask to use the radio-
phone. Since Mrs McIver was chatting with a
neighbour she told Ilona to go through and help
herself to the phone, adding that there were
instructions pinned up beside the instrument.

Eventually Ilona got through to the inn on the
mainland where Hugh had said he would book a
room, and the landlady fetched him to the phone.

'Hugh?' Ilona said hurriedly. 'Listen . . . I'm
taking full responsibility and giving you permission
to take pictures and measure, and whatever else it
is you have to do.'

'How am I going to get there without Lachlan
finding out?' Hugh asked doubtfully.

'Ask at the inn for an old man called Dougal,'
Ilona replied, watching rain drip like slow tears
down the steamy window of the little store-room.
'Then quietly ask him to tell you where you can
find a lad by the name of Donald Ogg. He's in the
habit of coming to Drumm uninvited and he'll
probably bring you. There's a landing-place on the
north side, a beach with a cave where you can put
your equipment. It's not far from the long barrow
and it's away from the houses and fields. I don't
think anybody goes there much.'

'It sounds ideal,' said Hugh, his voice warm
with enthusiasm. 'Will you come and see me?'

'Yes, I'll walk over that way—maybe in a day or
two. But Hugh, don't damage anything. Don't dig,
or make chalk marks, unless you tell me first.'

After a small silence he asked anxiously, 'Are
you risking trouble with Lachlan? I wouldn't want
that. Look, if by some chance he finds out I'm
there, I'll claim I came of my own accord, shall I?'

'No, don't lie for me, Hugh,' she replied. 'I

don't much care what Kyle thinks, or says, or does—not any more. I'm heir to half of Drumm, so I've as much right as he has to say who looks at that long barrow. I only hope it proves worth your trouble.'

'It will be,' he said. 'Thanks, Ilona. See you soon.'

As she put down the phone, Ilona laid a hand to her head, feeling depressed and thoroughly miserable. Yes, she did have every right to invite Hugh to come, but she wasn't very proud of herself, even if she was only playing Kyle tit for tat.

Returning through the little living room, she thanked Mrs McIver and bought a packet of mints from her store to eat on the long walk back to Creag Mhor.

But as she left the village, heading up the gentle slope between meadows, the Range Rover came bumping down the track towards her and stopped a few feet ahead. She saw Kyle lean across to open the passenger door.

'Mrs McTavish told me you'd gone out. Want a lift back?'

Ilona almost refused, but the rain poured down more determinedly than before and her shoes were already wet. Without looking at Kyle, she climbed up into the vehicle and closed the door before tossing back her hood to fluff her hair.

'I didn't know you liked walking in the rain,' Kyle remarked, sending the Range Rover into a U-turn which would take them back to Creag Mhor.

'There are a lot of things you don't know about me,' Ilona said stiffly. 'I fancied a breath of fresh air.'

'I would have thought you had enough of that this morning, up at the barrow with your Mr Danvers.'

Ilona took a deep breath, hating him. 'I went to phone my aunt, if you must know. And I bought some sweets.'

'Oh, yes? Are you going to offer me one?'

'No.'

In the ensuing silence, Kyle began to whistle tunelessly between his teeth, the sound grating along her raw nerves.

'Must you?' she said irritably, glancing at him for the first time. Which was a mistake, for so close to him in the confines of the vehicle she was captured by challenging grey eyes which had a deep furrow between them. She saw his tousled red hair, the strong column of his throat, and those lips that had called an irresistible response from her. Even now, when she knew him to be a liar and a cheat, he had the power to make her heartbeat quicken.

'Are you still annoyed with me for throwing Danvers off the island?' he demanded, returning his attention to the track.

'What do you think?' Ilona retorted.

'I think you might have asked me for my reasons.'

'I did—and you refused to give them to a spoilt, wilful child!'

He sighed heavily. 'Look, Ilona——'

'No!' she broke in. 'I'm not interested in your explanations. Hugh hadn't done anything to you.'

'Except for the fact that he used his acquaintance with you to come where he knew he wasn't wanted.'

'He came to see *me*.'

Once again he looked at her, with an intimate gaze that swept slowly over her dishevelled hair and every feature of her face before resting finally on her lips, making them tingle expectantly. She turned her head away so that he shouldn't see the way he made her feel, and saw that his inattention had taken them slightly off the bumpy track. They were heading for a scatter of rocks embedded in the ground.

'Kyle!' she cried.

'Blast it!' He slammed on the brakes, making the back of the Range Rover slew round in the wet grass.

As the vehicle stopped, still upright and intact, Ilona let out a long breath of relief, and Kyle began to swear under his breath, each word full of impotent exasperation.

'This can't go on,' he growled eventually. 'It's the damned uncertainty that's getting to me. You're determined to stay, are you? The full six months to claim your share?'

Ilona looked at him with bright green eyes, her mouth stubborn. 'I most certainly am.'

'Then it's about time we got something settled. I suggest we take a trip to Edinburgh and see the solicitor, to find out if that six-month clause is watertight. The sooner we get this whole thing on a proper legal basis, so that we both know exactly where we stand, the happier we shall both be.'

The proposition astounded Ilona. 'I'm supposed to stay on Drumm. It will invalidate my claim if I leave. Or is that your intention?'

He shot her a look of total disgust. 'If I had any such intentions I'd be a bit more subtle about it. One night isn't going to make any difference. I'll arrange it as soon as I can—make an appointment, book a hotel. A change might do us both good. This place is beginning to feel claustrophobic.'

So he felt it, too, Ilona thought as he reversed the vehicle and set it back on the track; he wasn't quite as insensitive as she had thought. She was, however, mystified by his motives for suggesting the trip. He couldn't be anxious to establish her rights as co-heir, not after he had tried so hard to prevent her from even coming to Drumm.

It had to have something to do with the oil. Perhaps he wanted to start the drilling during the summer, and with ownership in question there might be difficulties. Well, let him try it. She had every intention of baulking his plans to exploit Drumm.

CHAPTER SEVEN

A FEW days later, Ilona flew with Kyle to the
nearest airport on the mainland. A car waited for
them to drive the rest of the way to Edinburgh, on
a long road through purpling hills, past a myriad
blue lochs shining in the sun. Ilona had dressed in
a skirt suit with a pretty blouse, her hair fastened
up in a businesslike manner, while beside her Kyle
wore a sports jacket and rollneck sweater.

Neither of them were relaxed. Kyle's hands on
the driving wheel kept clenching until the knuckles
were white, and when Ilona glanced at him she
saw a muscle twitching in his jaw, as if he had his
teeth clenched. For herself, she felt breathless and
on edge from being so near him in the car.

Having stopped for lunch on the journey, they
reached Edinburgh by mid-afternoon. The city
whirled with traffic and pedestrians; tall grey
houses stood erect, and along Princes Street shops
looked out to the rock gardens which climbed the
foot of the crag on which the ancient Castle reared
its proud turrets, with flags flying.

'We shall just about make it in time for the
appointment,' said Kyle as he effortlessly guided
the car through streams of other vehicles.

But the meeting with Hamish McGregor's old
friend and legal adviser, Andrew McKay, proved
to be a waste of time. There was no way to alter
the terms of the will, he assured them; Ilona had to
spend six months on Drumm if she wanted to
claim her half of the inheritance, and until that

113

time was up—or until she chose to leave and give up her claim—everything must remain as it was.

Kyle argued, cajoled, lost his temper and finally said, 'Hell! Then we've wasted our time.'

Mr McKay looked at him through gold-rimmed spectacles beneath thick white hair. 'It certainly seems that way, Mr Lachlan. I'm sorry. But I've no doubt Hamish McGregor had good reasons for what he set down.'

'Oh, I'm sure he did,' Kyle growled, and got out of his chair to stroll restlessly to the window, where he stood rubbing the back of his neck.

The solicitor smiled at Ilona. 'How are you enjoying your stay on Drumm?'

'I love it,' she said with feeling. 'But perhaps, while we're here, you could tell me . . . If at some time either of us should wish to dispose of our share in the island, would it be possible to sell?'

'You're not thinking of . . .'

'Oh, no!' she said swiftly. 'But one never knows what may happen in the future. I mean . . . suppose, for instance, I were to get married, the chances are I would have to leave Drumm.'

'In which case you'd be entitled to half the capital,' Mr McKay told her. 'But if you did think of selling your share of the island, too, you couldn't do so without Mr Lachlan's agreement, and of course the same would be true should *he* wish to sell, or to make any major changes, in fact.'

'I see. Thank you.' She smiled brilliantly at him, well content. Kyle would not sell the island to a third party, or bring in oil wells to destroy its beauty, because she would simply refuse to agree to it. After all, it had not been a wasted journey.

They took their leave of the solicitor, Kyle terse

and breathing fury. He took Ilona's arm and all but forced her down the stairs and into the street, but he seemed too angry to voice his thoughts and she guessed that he didn't like having his plans impeded by a 'wilful child'.

When they reached the hotel, Kyle told Ilona he was going for a walk and would meet her in the bar at seven-thirty, for an aperitif before dinner.

Still riding on a wave of triumph, she ordered tea in her room and decided to take a look at the shops before they closed.

Not far from the hotel, the main shopping area offered a brilliant array of goods. Ilona window-shopped with no intention of buying, just passing the time and trying to take her mind off Kyle. Until, that was, she saw the dress.

It was displayed in the window of an elegant gown shop whose exclusiveness was declared by the fact that it showed no price tags. Ilona didn't dare wonder how much the dress would cost, but it was the kind of gown she had always dreamed of wearing, black and floaty, very simple with a silver motif embroidered down one side and a slim matching scarf affair to toss casually round one's neck to draw attention to the acres of tender skin revealed by a strapless top. Her head filled with dreams of wearing that dress, coming down the wide stairs at the hotel where her escort stood waiting, speechless with admiration. In her mind the man was Kyle and she didn't even wonder why that should be—why not Hugh, or some gorgeous stanger?

Behind the velvet curtains in the changing room, Ilona stared at her reflection. The dress showed most of the upper curve of her breasts and made her waist look tiny before it fell in soft folds to her feet, giving a tantalising hint of curves at hip and thigh. The black showed off her ivory skin and shining golden hair to perfection.

The assistant returned, to stand admiring the result. 'You look wonderful in that, madam.'

'It is lovely, isn't it?' Ilona said wistfully. 'How much is it?'

When the woman told her she almost fainted with shock. Heavens, that was more than her old monthly pay-cheque! But oh, she longed to own that dress. She did have some money put by in her bank account, and if only Kyle would see her as a woman then it would be worth it.

'I'll take it,' she said.

By seven-thirty she had bathed, made-up, done her hair in a fancy style with little curls trailing round her face and neck, and had donned the black dress. In the soft lights of the hotel room it looked even more alluring and her skin glowed softly, giving off a hint of heady perfume.

Ilona allowed herself to dream again, imagining Kyle's reaction when he saw her. But would he assume she was giving him the green light? The thought brought her back to earth and she stared in consternation at her reflection, knowing exactly what her aunt would have said. 'Really, Ilona, you're practically naked! And with your drawbacks you ought to know better. Those freckles—that wide mouth—and, my dear, you're almost buxom!'

Nearly in tears, Ilona tore herself away from the mirror, reaching for the fastener at the back of the dress intending to take it off and wear her prim primrose instead, but before she could do anything there came a knock at the door. Thinking that it must be the chambermaid, she went to answer the knock and stared blankly at Kyle's tall figure in an elegant dark suit, with a bow tie at the neck of a brilliant white shirt which made his tan seem mahogany-dark.

'I came to escort you down in case you got lost,' he told her. 'Are you ready?'

Distracted, Ilona glanced round the room, almost surprised to find that Aunt Zoe was not there, to see or criticise. 'Yes, I think so. I'll just get my bag.' Fate had decreed she wore the dress, it seemed, and she was too confused to figure out what might come of it.

Approaching Kyle again, she remembered that this was the moment she had dreamed about. She paused, letting him take a good look, but as far as she could tell the sight of her affected him much the same as if she had been a life-size doll.

She was forced to say it: 'What do you think?'

'You'll pass in a crowd,' he replied. 'Shall we go?'

Disappointment lanced through her like a pin deflating an overblown balloon. What had she expected? Compliments? From him?

All through dinner her mind kept wandering, going over events and conversations, memory bringing her alternate pain and pleasure. Afterwards she couldn't remember what they ate, though it seemed to be tasty and vastly expensive, accompanied by a cool dry wine of which she drank only two glasses. But that was enough to confuse her thoughts even further.

'You're not saying very much,' Kyle commented eventually. 'I thought you'd enjoy the evening, being in different surroundings. Is that a new dress?'

'Do you care?' she asked bitterly.

'If you're fishing for compliments,' Kyle returned, 'you're using the wrong bait.'

'I shall get all the compliments I need when Hugh Danvers sees me,' she flashed back. 'He knows how to treat a woman—with a little finesse, not head-on like a bull at a gate!'

'Thank you for the advice. I'll try to remember it.'

How, she wondered, could he sit there so calmly, being insufferable, and still make a part of her ache for him? While he poured himself more wine she watched him with veiled eyes. Hair redder than new chestnuts, unruly waves combed into as much order as they would ever agree to—his hair had a will of its own, like him. It would not be flattened into convention. Even now, elegant in a room full of elegant men, Kyle stood out because of that hair. He might dress his body in conservative clothing, but that flaming head would always mark him as different and no amount of tailored wool could disguise the breadth of his shoulders, his leanness of hip, or the easy way he moved on long, long legs. Wild. Barbarian. Most of the other women in the restaurant had noticed it, too; Ilona had seen their predatory looks as he passed.

She was thinking evil thoughts about those other women when Kyle looked across at her, the meeting of their glances sending a shockwave down to her toes. She was so vividly aware of him that each look seemed like a caress—a rough, uncaring, casual caress that wounded even while it excited her.

'Are you putting the evil eye on me?' he enquired with such cool scorn that she could have slapped him.

'I wasn't thinking about you at all,' she snapped.

'Then who was the cause of that daggers look? The immovable Mr McKay?'

Bewilderment showed in her eyes as she wondered what that could possibly mean. 'Why should I be annoyed with Mr McKay?'

'You tell me. Didn't he put paid to your plans?'

Into the middle of this one-sided discussion, a voice trilled, 'Kyle! Darling!' and Morag appeared at his elbow wearing a froth of lace on a green dress so tight that Ilona thought sourly that it made the tall, thin Morag resemble a snake. A snake in the grass, maybe.

'How lovely to see you!' Morag was carolling, one hand possessively on Kyle's shoulder as she smiled down at him. 'Imagine us both being in Edinburgh at the same time. I'm here doing interviews—boring, darling, but one must earn one's crust. And you?'

'Business with the solicitor,' Kyle said shortly, glancing at Ilona.

'Oh, I see.' Morag half turned as if to include Ilona in the conversation, managing at the same time to slide her hand behind Kyle's head, ruffling his hair. 'So that's why she's here, too. Something to do with the will?'

To Ilona's interested eyes, Kyle appeared to be uncomfortable with the intimate caresses Morag was giving him. He tossed his head and stood up abruptly, making the dark girl take her hand away from him. For some reason his irritation made Ilona want to giggle.

'If you've finished your dinner, darling,' said Morag, 'why don't we go and have a drink? It's ages since I saw you. I'd have been out to Drumm, but the journey's such a drag and I've been rushed off my feet with work. Oh—join us if you like, Miss McGregor.'

Ilona rose to her feet with conscious grace, smiling sweetly as if she were perfectly content when what she really wanted to do was ... well, something violent, something to wipe that smug grin off Morag's face.

'Three's a crowd, as they say,' she replied. 'I'll go up to my room, I think.'

'Yes, you do look a bit tired,' said Morag with every appearance of concern. 'Goodnight. Sweet dreams.'

In her room, Ilona kicked off her shoes, tore off the beautiful dress and left it in a bedraggled heap before scrubbing her face clean of every trace of make-up. She put on a silky robe, tied the belt tightly, then unpinned her hair and brushed it out with swift, angry strokes, unable to face herself in the mirror. Everything had gone wrong. So much for dreams. Though why on earth she had ever dreamed of a rosily romantic evening with Kyle Lachlan she could not imagine. He was everything she detested in a man—arrogant, brutal, scheming. The one thing that had been in his favour had been his caring for Drumm, but even that illusion had vanished when she found out that all he really cared about was the oil deposits.

And now Morag had come and claimed him! It was too much!

Torn apart by the war of her emotions, she flung herself down on the bed and gave way to tears.

Some time later, a soft tap on the door made her sit up. The sound came again, more insistently, and Ilona slid off the bed, drying her face as she moved to the door, and asked, 'Who is it?'

'Kyle,' the answer came quietly. 'May I speak to you, just for a minute?'

Straightening her hair with her fingers, Ilona opened the door a few inches. 'What about?'

'I wanted to apologise for . . .' he began, and stopped to frown down at her. 'Have you been crying?'

'No, not really,' she replied, knowing that her voice, her reddened eyes and her tear-streaked face proclaimed her a liar.

Kyle glanced along the corridor, where a procession of people seemed to have chosen that moment to come and go from their rooms. Sighing heavily, he leaned on the doorjamb to murmur, 'We can't talk like this. May I come in? I promise to behave.'

'If you want to,' she shrugged, moving away to sit by the dressing-mirror and brush her hair, trying to give the impression of casual ease when all her pulses were thudding at top speed.

Closing the door, Kyle came to stand where he could see her through the mirror. Ilona kept her eyes fixed on her own reflection, though she could see his dark figure behind her and was appalled by the tear-marks on her face.

'Are you going to tell me what's wrong?' he asked.

'Nothing's wrong.'

'Ilona!' He grasped her by the shoulders and swung her round to face him, bending over her with a frown. 'Don't lie to me. You were upset when I called for you earlier. You've been monosyllabic all through dinner, and now you've been crying. Why?'

'Why should I tell you?' she cried, coming to her

feet with a rush that almost unbalanced him as she put several feet between them. 'You don't care. You don't care about anything—not Drumm, not anything. Go back to your girl-friend and leave me alone!'

'Not until you tell me what's wrong! What happened after we got here? You were all right until then.'

'I'd be all right now if only you would go away!'

Two huge strides brought him to her side. His hands shot out and fastened on to her shoulders, shaking her so that her hair tossed over her face. 'Stop this, Ilona! Stop it! You're hysterical!'

Wide terrified eyes dazzled with tears stared up at him and she trembled visibly in his hands.

'Ilona . . .' He sounded almost worried. 'Are you so afraid of me? I wouldn't hurt you.'

'You're always hurting me!' she managed, turning her head away. Yes, she was afraid, but mostly of the effect he was having on her physically. She wanted desperately to wilt against him and fold her arms round his lean body.

'I don't mean to,' he told her, his fingers rubbing her shoulders as if to comfort her. 'But why do you always fight me? Come here, little mermaid.'

She found herself exactly where she longed to be—where she had dreaded being—folded closely in his arms with her face against that soft white shirt, where she could hear his heart hammering. Closing her eyes tightly, she fought the desire to lean against his strength, her hands clenched in front of her to keep him that small distance away, but his fingers slipped through her hair and a long thumb lifted her chin.

'Kyle!' she protested, but her resistance collapsed as his lips claimed hers with masterful passion, taking her spinning down into a whirlpool of delight, like drowning, like the way they had met, and almost as dangerous. Without conscious volition her hands crept up his jacket and locked behind his neck, her fingers exploring the silky texture of that wild red hair. Her lips parted and she uttered a sigh, giving herself totally to the answering of a need that had been growing in her for too long.

'Why do you fight me?' he muttered, his breath warm in her ear. 'I want you—I've wanted you for weeks. This is the way Hamish intended us to be.'

Warm kisses pressed across her face, reaching her all-too-willing mouth again, while his hands caressed her through the thin robe, exploring the contours of shoulderblades and the length of her spine, moving round to her ribs. She felt the belt of her robe come undone and Kyle's hand shook as he found her breast, making her shudder and moan as a flame began to burn deep within her, sending her further towards total abandon.

When he lifted her bodily into his arms she buried her face against his throat, her lips nibbling his flesh. He laid her on the bed and paused to throw off his jacket and tie and unbutton his shirt, while she watched him with languorous eyes, seeing his gaze devour her uncovered body, his own eyes darkened by desire.

'You're beautiful,' he told her gruffly. 'In that dress you were stunning, but without it . . .'

'Why didn't you tell me so?' she asked, holding out her arms as he lay beside her.

'I was annoyed with you. And then I wondered why you were upset. Did I make you unhappy?

Dear little mermaid . . .' His fingers ran over her,
light as butterfly kisses, calling fresh tremors from
depths she had not guessed were part of her. He
kissed her mouth and let his lips trace a slow,
devastating pathway down her throat to the soft
valley between her breasts, while Ilona caressed his
hair and strong warm shoulders.

'Forget Hugh Danvers,' he muttered, rousing
her with tiny kisses across her taut breasts. 'You're
mine. You've been mine since I took you from the
sea. In the restaurant tonight I could have killed
all those men who kept watching you. I wanted to
cover you up and take you back to Drumm, where
only I could see you. Hamish meant us to get
together, Ilona.'

He lifted himself so that he could look down at
her, into green eyes as soft as summer seas. 'Marry
me, Ilona. Dearest Ilona . . .'

His lips found hers again, achingly soft and then
hardening, demanding. His fingers drew circles on
her body, across her ribs and her stomach, to her
hip . . .

Ilona gasped, half afraid and half excited almost
beyond endurance. But it would be all right.
Marry me . . . that was what he had said. Not even
Aunt Zoe could object to that.

But he hadn't said he loved her. 'I want you,'
and 'You're mine,' and 'Hamish intended it,' but
not, 'I love you.'

He drew back, fumbling with the waistband of
his trousers, and Ilona pulled the robe to hide her
nakedness. Desire . . . she thought. Lust, without
love. Oh, he could be pleasant now, when he
wanted something of her. He could be tender and
speak sweet words, but it was Drumm that was on
his mind—Drumm and the riches it would bring.

Smiling, Kyle reached to uncover her again. 'Don't be shy with me. You're going to be my wife, remember?'

She fended his hand away and sat up with her back turned to him. 'Is that how you persuaded Morag to sleep with you?'

'Darling!' he said softly, amused. 'Morag isn't . . .'

As his hand touched her shoulder, Ilona leapt away and whirled to face him, wrapping the robe securely about her as her eyes blazed in a face gone deathly pale. 'Morag told me you were going to marry *her*. How many other girls have you seduced with that trick?'

Kyle stared at her, kneeling on the bed naked to the waist, his surprise hardening into anger. Anger at being thwarted by her again, she thought bitterly. He believed that if he made love to her she would not oppose his plans for Drumm. Perhaps he really meant to marry her, since as her husband he could claim full rights over the island. He had tried everything else, hadn't he? Tried buying her off and frightening her away. Now he used the ultimate betrayal, her own body.

'You said you would behave yourself,' she reminded him hoarsely.

'That's what I was doing,' he grated. 'Behaving as I thought you wanted me to behave. You gave a good impression of being as eager as I was.'

Knowing it to be the truth, she flushed with shame. 'Get out of my room, Kyle. Let's have no more play-acting. You've made a mistake if you think I can be bought off with words. Whatever you do, I'll fight you. And if you touch me again I swear I'll scream and make such a fuss that you'll get your name in every paper in Scotland!'

With a growl of rage he swung off the bed away from her, threw on his shirt and bent to snatch up his jacket and tie before glowering at her. 'That's the way of it, is it? You've spent all evening giving me the come-on and now you'd cry rape. I don't mind a woman who's cold as ice—that I can understand. But a woman who's cold and a tease—that's the lowest form of female I can think of!'

'And the lowest form of man is one who'd make love to a woman for his own gain!' she cried. 'Great-uncle Hamish guessed wrong in more ways than one. But I intend to set that straight. I'll make you an offer—I'll buy your share of Drumm.'

Kyle's brows came down in a black frown beneath which his eyes glimmered like icicles. 'So that's your game! You think you can get rid of me, do you? Well, you may as well know that I wouldn't sell to you if you could actually raise what Drumm is worth to me—which is beyond calculation. It's *my* home, and nobody's going to dispossess me!'

The door slammed behind him deafeningly. Shaking, Ilona sat down on the rumpled bed, feeling sick of herself. How nearly she had let him make love to her. How badly she had wanted it—still wanted it, if she was honest with herself. And that for a man who had only money on his mind. Dear God, would she never be able to look at him with indifference?

The silence between them now crackled with ice-cold hostility. All the way back to Drumm, Ilona was obliged to sit beside Kyle, aware of the power of him, wanting to talk to him openly as she had done during those weeks before Hugh Danvers arrived. But how did one talk to a deceiver? How could one ever be sure what was truth and what was lies? Safer not to talk at all. Safer not even to look at him and risk being enchanted by those rugged looks and hypnotic grey eyes.

They arrived at Creag Mhor in plenty of time for dinner, but when Ilona presented herself in the dining room she was told by Mrs McTavish that Kyle had discovered some problem waiting for him, so he had elected to eat in the study. Not at all surprised, Ilona sat down to her own lonely meal.

'I went down to the harbour yesterday morning,' the housekeeper vouchsafed as she served a slice of peach flan. 'Och, you should hear the tales that are going round on account of that legend! It was your friend Mr Danvers arriving like that.'

'Like what?' Ilona asked sharply.

'Why, on the provision boat, dearie. How else should I mean? Anyway, they're all talking about it. "The dark-haired man who is not of the island".' She rolled her eyes and laughed. 'Alice McVeigh swears blind he'll be back to carry you off.'

'Well, she needn't worry,' Ilona replied. 'I have no intention of leaving—with Hugh Danvers or anyone else. I'm beginning to feel I belong here.'

'Aye, dearie,' Mrs McTavish said fondly. 'We feel the same. It's just grand to have a McGregor here again.'

Quite whom she meant by 'we' was not clear, but Ilona didn't think the plural included Kyle. In one respect, however, the gossip was probably correct—by now the 'dark-haired man' probably was on the island. Ilona only hoped he had left no traces of his investigations.

Unable to settle after dinner, mainly for fear of Kyle's emerging from his study to continue the silent war, Ilona set off for a walk, thinking it would help her sleep. At that time of year the night came late to the isles and the sky was still ablaze with scarlet afterglow as Ilona walked steadily across the purple heather, seeing the lambs grown fat and hearing the gulls cry their mournful song as they swam through the bright twilight.

Truly Drumm was beautiful, Ilona thought. In all its moods, whether sombre, stormy or bright. Like its Laird. But she mustn't start thinking that way, not again. Her senses must learn to obey her logical mind, not her stupid susceptible heart.

Dusk began to feather across the world as she approached the highest point on the island, where the standing stones looked like giant figures in the half-light. Beyond them a three-quarter moon began to gleam in the darkening sky and stars blinked on one by one.

To Ilona's annoyance, she found the barrow measured off in sections with small markers which remained in the ground. It was careless of Hugh to leave so much evidence of his visits. Suppose Kyle found the markers?

'I was hoping you'd come.'

The voice made her jump and she looked up to see a shadow detach itself from the darkness near one of the stones. For a second she thought it was Kyle—he was that close to the centre of her mind—then she realised that this man was less tall, less broad, and the moon shone on dark hair.

Hugh laughed as he strolled towards her. 'Did I startle you?'

'I thought you'd have gone long ago,' said Ilona, 'Does Donald Ogg sail in the dark?'

'I hardly trust him even in broad daylight. He's too fond of dicing with death on the rocks—which is apparently why Lachlan told him to stay clear. He brought me out a couple of times, but then I hired myself some equipment, and an outboard, and now I'm camping in your cave. I've been waiting for you to come.'

'I've been busy,' she replied. 'We went to Edinburgh.'

'We?'

'Kyle and I.'

'I see.'

She could not see his face clearly, but his voice told her enough. 'On business!' she said sharply.

'I'm glad to hear it.' Smiling, he moved closer and looped his arms round her waist. 'So, here you are. On a warm moonlit night. Romantic, isn't it?'

Ilona tried to move away, but his hands were locked behind her and she was caught in the circle. 'Those markers . . .' she said. 'Do they have to stay here?'

'Until I've finished my work, yes. My dear ignoramus, I can't re-measure every day, now can I?'

'But how long is it going to take?'

'Oh, another few days—it can't be done in a rush. Let's not talk about that. I've been lonely without you. Have I told you you've grown into a lovely lady?'

His arms suddenly clasped round her, bringing her full against him, and he kissed her on the mouth rather awkwardly. Ilona braced herself to struggle, but hesitated, hoping that Hugh might break that spell which Kyle had woven round her heart. But all she felt was a rising revulsion at his clumsiness and the smell of whisky on his breath. Three years before she hadn't known the difference, but now she had been kissed by Kyle Lachlan, who was undoubtedly an expert, and Hugh's hamfisted pawings sickened her.

Just as she was about to force him away, he let her go, grinning so widely that he couldn't have noticed her lack of response to him. 'You'll take my mind off my work,' he said. 'I was just taking a stroll before turning in. Unless you'd care to come down to my bivouac for a nightcap. I've got a bottle of whisky.'

'No, thanks,' said Ilona. 'I'd better get back. Just be sure not to disturb anything, Hugh.'

As swiftly as the moonlight would allow, she returned to Creag Mhor and went immediately to the bathroom to take a hot shower in an effort to rid herself of the feel of Hugh's lips and hands. She felt soiled, which was odd. She never felt that way after Kyle had touched her. But it was clear to her now that all Hugh cared about was the barrow.

One thing she was glad to know, though—Kyle had no sinister reason for barring Donald Ogg from Drumm. She only wished his motives for other actions had been as innocuous.

The following morning she woke to find a mist blanketing the island. Wearing only a flimsy nightdress, she knelt on the windowseat and looked out at the grey veil that all but hid the shore of the loch. It suited her melancholy mood. If only she could find some understanding with Kyle . . .

Oh, Kyle! She leaned her forehead against the

cold windowpane, filled with a misery she did not comprehend.

Behind her, the door flung open, crashing into a chair. Ilona spun round and stared in outrage at the frowning Kyle, who stood arms akimbo in the doorway, clad in tight-fitting jeans with his torso only half concealed by a plaid shirt that was open to the waist.

'Kyle! What do you mean by——' The sentence choked off as she realised her state of undress. The nightgown was as transparent as the mist outside and Kyle slowly let his cool gaze drink in the sight of every inch of her.

A hot flush began at Ilona's bare feet and travelled up her body, flooding her face with colour as she grabbed her dressing gown and held it draped in front of her, shaking back her tousled hair to regard him mutinously.

'What do you want? What gives you the right to burst in here and . . . Stop looking at me!'

A slow, cold smile curved his mouth. 'I'm a man who appreciates a lovely view—you should know that by now. But you needn't look so horrified. I'm not about to leap on you, even though you sorely tempt me.'

'You're disgusting!' Ilona spat. 'Can't you think about anything else?'

'I do keep trying, I assure you. But the other women on Drumm are too old or too young. There's only you . . .' His eyes were roaming again.

'Stop it, Kyle!'

He grimaced with disgust, flicking his gaze back to her face. 'What a pity the only woman available is such a cold fish. But I didn't come here to discuss my libido. I wondered if you might be interested in taking a little walk with me.'

'A walk to where?'

'To the long barrow. I'm going to put your friend Danvers off this island. And this time I'll make sure he never comes back.'

Stricken, Ilona found herself staring at an empty doorway. How did he know about Hugh?

'Kyle!' She ran out to the landing, but he had gone down the circular stairs. 'Kyle!!'

'You'd better get dressed in a hurry,' his voice floated back. 'I'm on my way now.'

CHAPTER EIGHT

THROWING on some clothes, Ilona fled down the stairs. Mrs McTavish was in the hall, saying with some surprise, 'Why, Miss Ilona, don't you want any breakfast?'

'Later,' Ilona gasped.

Despite the mist the day was not cold but rather warm and muggy. There was no sign of Kyle, though she hadn't expected him to be waiting. She scrambled up the hillside and began to run across the uneven ground.

Long before she reached the barrow her pace had slowed. She was out of breath and had a pain in her side—'the stitch', she thought forlornly, remembering the childhood phrase. It forced her to a walk, and all the time her mind kept playing mental videos of what might be happening at the barrow. Would Kyle be content with verbal abuse, or would he lose his head and become violent? She had visions of Hugh being pushed off the cliff on to the rocks below. And then Kyle would be in trouble. Don't lose your temper, Kyle! she prayed. Please don't.

At last she reached the place and leaned on one of the megaliths to get her breath. The long barrow lay silent, but Hugh's markers were all flattened, as if someone had trampled on them. Where had the men gone? What had happened between them?

Remembering that Hugh had been camping in the cave, Ilona forced her shaking muscles to carry

133

her further, finding the path that led to the north corner of the island. Through the heavy grey veil that hung in the air white birds came winging, screeching at her, a whole flurry of them warning her away from their nests.

Clambering down among the rocks, she saw the cave mouth as a black shape through the mist, and by it two figures stood—Kyle with his legs planted apart and his thumbs hooked in the loops of his belt, his whole demeanour arrogantly masterful, while Hugh carried something from the cave towards a small boat pulled up on the beach. Not far away the sea churned, slate-grey waves rolling heavily to throw spume high in the air as they crashed on the rocks.

Kyle looked at her expressionlessly, his face as human as carved granite, red curls moving on his furrowed brow. Glancing to where Hugh was stowing his equipment in the boat, Ilona demanded, 'Who told you he was here?'

'I know everything that goes on on Drumm,' Kyle said evenly. 'At least, I eventually find out everything. I should have listened to the islanders, shouldn't I? They kept telling me the 'dark-haired man' would come back.'

Rocks crunched beneath Hugh's feet as he returned, his face pale and set. He was leaving, but only under protest. 'Don't you worry about this, Ilona,' he said quietly, touching her arm. 'This is between him and me. I'm going in order to save any more trouble, but I won't be far away. Any time you want me, send for me and I'll come, whether he likes it or not.'

'On a white charger, no doubt,' said Kyle with a sharp laugh. 'Or will you actually turn into a black water-horse?'

The reference mystified Hugh, who looked to Ilona for explanations, but she shrugged and said, 'It doesn't matter—take no notice. Hugh, I'm sorry.'

'For what?' he asked. 'None of this is your fault, love. Just you remember that I'll be on hand if you need me. If he tries anything . . .'

'You're scaring me to death,' Kyle broke in sardonically. 'Get on with it, Danvers, your time's running out.'

Hugh's mouth tightened, but he moved away to the cave to fetch the last bundle of his belongings.

'What gives you the right to do this, Kyle?' Ilona demanded. 'He hasn't done any harm.'

He folded his arms across his opened shirt, staring at her through his lashes. 'What gave you the right to ask him to come back?'

She caught her breath. 'How did you know——'

'He told me,' he said with a dismissive flick of his head at Hugh. 'A fine champion you've got there! The minute I appeared on the scene he started making excuses, saying it wasn't his fault, it was yours. You told him how to get here and Donald Ogg brought him.'

Coming past them, Hugh caught the drift of the conversation and said tightly, 'She told me not to lie.'

'And I suppose,' said Kyle, 'that you always do what a woman tells you, even if it means letting her down.'

'You're not worth arguing with,' Hugh said with disgust, making for the boat. 'You'd better come and give me a hand to get this launched, if you want me to leave.'

'With pleasure,' Kyle replied.

Ilona followed them, wondering how they were

going to manage to launch that frail craft through seas that boiled over boulders. The tide appeared to be on the turn.

'You can't make him go in this weather!' she protested.

'It was his choice,' said Kyle. 'I offered to go with him, or even take him in the chopper and bring the boat later, but he reckons he can handle it alone.'

'Of course I can handle it,' Hugh retorted. 'I'll handle it if it kills me. Sooner that than ask *you* for help, Lachlan.'

'But it's dangerous!' Ilona exclaimed, her ears full of the thunder of the surf.

Her warning went unheeded. The boat scraped across the rocks as the two men dragged it towards the water, both of them getting soaked to the waist before the craft bobbed free, twisting and turning as Hugh climbed aboard and all but fell into the seat. While Kyle employed all his considerable strength to hold the boat steady, Hugh struggled with the outboard. Three times it choked and gasped in the humid air before the engine caught and Hugh grasped the tiller, turning it towards the open sea.

' 'Bye, Ilona!' his call came above the roar of the sea and the chuckle of the motor. 'Don't forget . . .' But whatever it was that she mustn't forget was lost in the tumult of sound.

As Kyle stepped up onto a big rock away from the water, Ilona watched the boat with fear-quickened senses. It was being tossed on the breakers, the engine making little leeway against the power of the ocean, and Hugh's free hand clenched grimly on the gunwale.

'He'll never make it!' she yelled at Kyle.

'He said he could,' he returned. '*I* could make it, and so could Donald Ogg.'

'But you're used to these waters! Hugh isn't a sailor. Haven't you got any feelings at——'

She stopped as a sharp cry alerted her to Hugh's danger. Above a foam-crested wave she saw the bow of the boat flip skywards, side on to the seas. For a moment it seemed to hang there, then Hugh vanished in a flurry of spray. The boat landed upside down.

'Kyle!' Her scream echoed round the cliffs, mocked by the cries of seabirds. She clapped her hands to her ears, wanting to cover her eyes but knowing she must watch. This was all her fault.

Hugh's head broke surface. He shouted for help as he floundered, then he was submerged by another wave.

'Hold those!' Kyle yelled, and as she looked at him his shoes came hurtling through the air. She grabbed for them, catching one as he stepped into the foam, striding through waves that crashed against his knees, then his waist, before he dived into the tumultuous water and struck out strongly.

'Help me!' Hugh's call came again, but both of the men were lost to sight among the heaving waves. All Ilona could see was the occasional glimpse of a head and arms. First she lost Hugh, then she lost Kyle.

She stood rigidly, clutching Kyle's shoe to her and praying desperately for divine aid.

Suddenly she saw them again, together now several yards down the beach. A huge wave brought them closer inshore and she saw a dark figure stagger from the water, dragging another with him. Both of them collapsed against the rocks, bare inches from the ravening sea that seemed to howl with displeasure at being robbed.

Cursing the boulders that made her feet slow, Ilona hastened to the spot and found both men gasping for breath, water running from their clothes and hair.

'Kyle!' she breathed, but it was Hugh she bent over, since he was nearest and seemed the worse for his experience. 'Hugh, can you hear me?'

'Give him a minute!' Kyle croaked, pushing himself to his knees and shaking himself in dog-like fashion, spattering water over her. 'He'll live. But don't just stand there, woman! Go and get help. I think your boy-friend's broken his arm.'

Never had the island seemed so large. It seemed to take her hours to climb the cliff path and race across the heather-clad uplands. She was all but incoherent with breathlessness by the time she scrambled down the final slope to Creag Mhor and saw Mrs McTavish emerge from the back door.

'Why, dearie!' the housekeeper exclaimed. 'Whatever's wrong?'

'An accident,' Ilona gasped. 'Hugh Danvers . . . Kyle thinks his arm's broken. He's unconscious. What shall we do?'

'First of all, we stay calm,' said Mrs McTavish severely. 'Now, do you drive?'

'Yes, but why——'

'Then you can take the Range Rover. We'll get the stretcher out of the helicopter and put it in the back of the car, with the medical bag, and then you drive back through the village and get one of the men to go with you—Mr Lachlan'll need help carrying the stretcher.'

At the time, the convenient coincidence of the availability of a stretcher and medical equipment did not strike Ilona as odd. She was all too glad that the problem could be solved so easily.

Between them, she and Mrs McTavish got the things into the Range Rover and Ilona set out, taking the steep path slowly until she reached the summit behind the castle, then her foot pressed down hard on the accelerator as the vehicle bucked across the track. Her heart hammered uncomfortably as she wondered what could be happening back at the beach. Suppose Hugh was seriously injured?

Before she reached the village, she saw a sturdy figure emerge out of the mist, walking towards her with a collie dog at his heels. Relieved, Ilona stopped the car and rolled down her window.

'Mr McIver! Mr McIver, can you help me, please? There's been an accident. By the cave. We may need help with the stretcher.'

Jock McIver needed no persuasion but immediately strode round to the passenger door and plumped himself down beside her, calling his dog to jump in and sit by his feet. A few short questions were all the shepherd asked as they bumped away, heading up the hillside for the far corner of Drumm.

Leaving the car at the cliff-top, they set off down through the mist, Jock McIver bringing the stretcher while Ilona followed with the heavy medical bag. At sight of the black and white collie the gulls went mad, diving and wheeling, but a word from the shepherd made the dog go on, its tail waving like a white-tipped flag as it went nimbly down among the rocks.

'That way,' said Ilona, pointing through the

mist, but as she spoke Kyle appeared through the grey fronds like some sea-spirit, his clothes soaked and clinging to his muscular frame, his red hair flattened to his skull around a face that held no trace of softness.

Shivering, he said, 'Where the hell have you been?' and relieved her of the bag, adding, 'Thanks, Jock. I'll need some help.'

No thanks for her, Ilona noted irritably as she negotiated the rocks to where Hugh lay.

He was conscious now, gritting his teeth as Kyle knelt to bind his arm tightly to his side. He protested that there was no need for the stretcher, that he could walk as far as the Range Rover, though when he stood up he was none too steady and his face went ashen. Kyle was obliged to support him back up the cliff.

The journey back to Creag Mhor was a slow one, with Kyle driving the Range Rover while Ilona sat in the back beside a shuddering Hugh, who gasped and moaned at every bump of the wheels. Occasionally, through the driving mirror, Ilona caught the bright, furious glint in Kyle's eyes and knew that he held her entirely to blame for what had happened. Which really wasn't fair. She still didn't understand why he was so super-possessive over the long barrow. And it was Hugh himself who had chosen to leave by boat. So why did Kyle direct all his anger at *her*?

As the helicopter lifted from its pad, braving the misty day, Ilona stood with Mrs McTavish to watch the machine clatter into the air and move away across the loch until it was hidden by the sea-fret.

'Don't you worry, dearie,' the housekeeper

comforted. 'He'll soon be in hospital and his arm looked after.'

'Yes, I know.' The events of the morning had left her emotionally and physically drained. 'At least Kyle seemed to know exactly what to do.'

'Well, he's had plenty of experience. Injuries and illnesses, pregnant women. He even delivered a baby once, when he got there too late to take the mother to hospital.'

'Kyle did?' exclaimed Ilona in astonishment. 'You mean the helicopter's a . . . an ambulance service?'

Mrs McTavish looked at her in surprise. 'Didn't you know that? I took it for granted Mr Lachlan would have told you. But he probably didn't want to boast about it. It was his idea, you see. There's no sort of emergency help provided for the islands, so if someone gets seriously ill they have to send for a naval helicopter, and it all takes time. Mr Lachlan persuaded Mr McGregor to buy a machine for the purpose. As soon as a call comes, he's off, anywhere he's needed—across the islands and sometimes on the mainland, if some lonely crofter needs help.'

'I see,' said Ilona faintly. This, then, was the answer to the irregular comings and goings of the helicopter. Altruism at its best, and Kyle was to thank for it. He was a man of strange contrasts.

But he hadn't been very altruistic with Hugh. He had been utterly arrogant and unfeeling, for reasons which Ilona did not understand. She herself felt partly responsible for the débâcle, but did Kyle feel the slightest guilt for Hugh's accident and the loss of his equipment? He had lost no time in racing indoors to change his clothes before flying out with Hugh, but he had spoken barely a word.

When they heard the helicopter returning, over an hour later, Mrs McTavish prepared some coffee to greet Kyle. Ilona waited in the small sitting room, curled up in a corner of the settee with the refreshments on a small table in front of her, and her mind replayed that scene on the beach for the hundredth time. She relived her fright when the boat had overturned and her sheer numbing terror when both men appeared to be lost.

Had it been that way on the day she arrived? Had Kyle been exhausted after risking his life to save her? She vaguely recalled being lifted, being held safe and secure against him, but until that moment she had not appreciated how it must have been for him. Now he had saved two lives—of two people he detested.

He came in still wearing the thick sweater and tweed slacks he had thrown on in such haste. Without a glance at Ilona he sat down in an armchair and leaned to switch on a bar of the electric fire.

'He'll be all right,' he told her. 'No damage apart from a clean break in his forearm. They'll keep him in for a few days and then . . .' He hesitated, a muscle jumping in his jaw as he gritted his teeth. 'He said he'd be going back to the inn for a while. Apparently he's still got some leave to come. And he sent you his love.' As he flatly conveyed the message he glanced at her from the corner of his eye, but immediately looked away again.

'I'm glad it wasn't worse,' Ilona said. 'We were all to blame, all three of us. How are you feeling?'

'I'm fine,' he said tonelessly.

When she handed him a cup of coffee he avoided her eyes, sitting forward in his chair with elbows on knees, his head bent so that she couldn't see his face clearly, and she sensed that he was ashamed of his behaviour that day. Shame, in him, was something new to Ilona, but she knew that she and Hugh had been equally responsible. A weakening wave of emotion ran through her and she had an urge to go to him, to put her arms round him and hold him close.

'But for you,' she reminded him softly, 'he'd have drowned.'

'But for me.' He laughed without humour and stared down into his coffee. 'But for me he'd have stayed on the island and you could have continued your secret starlight encounters.'

She caught her breath and, hearing it, Kyle looked at her with a derisory glint in his eye. 'I followed you last night. I had some crazy idea of . . . oh, I don't know what I might have done. And then I saw you wrapped cosily in Danvers' arms. I could hardly interrupt such a romantic scene.'

The scorn in his voice made her mouth set and her eyes grow stormy. 'I didn't think you'd sink to spying on me. I only told Hugh to come because you were being so unreasonable. You've got a fixation about that long barrow.'

'That long barrow,' he said levelly, 'is sacred ground as far as I'm concerned. Hamish thought the dead should lie in peace and he made me swear not to let it be disturbed as long as I lived. And if you really want to know why I was so angry . . .' He drained his coffee in one long gulp and stood up, cracking the cup back into the saucer.

'Well?' Ilona prompted.

He took a deep breath, a shudder running visibly through him. 'Hamish was cremated. He asked for his ashes to be scattered on the barrow. I did it myself.'

A ripple of horror ran down her spine. 'Why ever didn't you tell me that before?'

'I didn't want to distress you.' As he turned to place his cup on the table the muscle twitched again in his jaw. 'Stupid of me. For some reason I thought you'd feel as badly about Hamish's death as I did. I forgot you didn't even know him, or care about him.'

'I wasn't even sure he existed!' she protested. 'If you'd told me, I wouldn't have let Hugh go anywhere near the long barrow. It shan't be touched again, Kyle, I promise you. You ... you were very close to Hamish, weren't you? I didn't realise how much it had affected you. Did you know him for a long time?'

'Thirty years.'

Bewildered, Ilona did sums in her head. That wasn't possible. Even if Kyle had come to Drumm straight from college he could only have been factor for ten years or so.

His eyes looked bright but she couldn't read any expression in them. 'Since I was three years old,' he said in an undertone, and without haste he left the room.

He couldn't have stunned her more if he had slapped her.

Ilona went in search of Mrs McTavish to ask her for explanations, but the housekeeper was strangely reluctant to talk about Kyle's relationship with Hamish McGregor.

'The story's not mine to tell,' she said. 'But this I'll say—Mr Lachlan's mother was housekeeper here before me. He grew up in this house. Is there any wonder he feels as if he belongs here?'

No wonder at all, Ilona thought. Why hadn't anyone told her before now?

That evening when the mist closed in more thickly Ilona sat by the fire in the great hall waiting for Kyle to come home. The time had come, she thought, for her to tackle him about those reports of oil-bearing deposits, and to ask him more about his relationship with her great-uncle. She had begun to appreciate that he had had good reasons for resenting her intrusion on the island, but if he had been so fond of Hamish McGregor surely he ought to respect the old man's last wishes?

When at last Kyle came in, crashing the main door shut behind him, she was surprised to see him unsteady on his feet as he made for the stairs.

'Kyle?'

He stopped, one hand on the end of the banister half supporting himself, the other holding his head. Ilona hurried across to him, wondering what could be wrong.

'Kyle, I've got to talk to you.'

He swung round, swaying, blinking owlishly at her. 'Talk? It's not talking I'd like to do with you, you little——'

'You're drunk!' she exclaimed in disgust, stepping away.

'Drunk?' he repeated in a quiet, menacing tone. 'No.'

'I can smell it on your breath!'

'One dram was all I had, out of Jock McIver's flask,' he told her, a shudder running through him. 'God, it's cold in here! Leave me alone, woman. I must get changed for dinner.'

Frowning to herself, Ilona watched as he climbed the stairs, stumbling a little as he went.

One dram? she thought. And the rest! Clearly there would be no talking to him that night, not when he was in that state.

She did not enjoy the prospect of having dinner with him, but all the same she waited, sipping a small sherry to bolster her own courage. Mrs McTavish appeared to see if she should serve the dinner, but decided to wait a while, too. Fifteen endless minutes ticked by.

'It's not like him to be late for his meals,' the housekeeper said worriedly. 'Was he all right when he came in?'

'Apart from the fact that he appeared to have been celebrating—or drowning his sorrows,' Ilona told her, fairly sure that it had been the latter. Kyle had been in a strange mood all day.

Mrs McTavish looked at her as if she had taken leave of her senses. 'A dram too much, you mean? Why, that's not like Mr Lachlan. Maybe I should go and see what's keeping him.'

'Yes, perhaps you should.'

Worried now, she stood at the foot of the stairs waiting for the housekeeper to return and tell her what was going on. Mrs McTavish seemed to be a long time in Kyle's room, and eventually Ilona began to climb the stairs, fearing that Kyle might have hurt himself.

As she reached the gallery, Mrs McTavish emerged, flushed and breathing hard. 'Drunk, indeed!' she gasped. 'He's sick—he's burning up with fever. I've put him to bed. Would you credit it, he was trying to put on his best suit, the daft man. The state he was in!'

'Shall I go and——' Ilona began.

'No, lassie,' the housekeeper said at once, a firm arm barring Ilona's way. 'Best you stay clear for now. I'll tend to him. If you'd help me by getting your own dinner, I'd be obliged.'

Although she had never felt less like eating, Ilona forced down some food, but her mind was on the comings and goings of the housekeeper, up and down stairs carrying bowls and potions, with long interludes when she disappeared into Kyle's room.

'Can't I do something?' Ilona asked at one point. 'I feel so useless. Should we call a doctor?'

'No, no, I can cope, don't you fret. It's just a chill he's caught, after that soaking. He's been working too hard, and not eating properly. I knew it would end in grief.'

'But I'd be happy to sit with him if——'

'Lassie,' said Mrs McTavish with a frown, 'you'll help me best by staying away. He's not himself—he's rambling. Best leave it to me.'

The evening wore on and the late darkness came, while Ilona sat disconsolately by the fire with her mind on the room upstairs. She could not understand why she was so firmly excluded when Mrs McTavish seemed to be run off her feet. She wanted to help. She wanted to see Kyle. How blind she had been to think him drunk when actually he had been ill!

'He's sleeping now,' the housekeeper said eventually. 'We'll leave him to his rest and hope the morning brings better things.'

Unhappily, Ilona took herself to bed, but sleep was a long time coming and when the early dawn brought gulls crying round her window she got up and slipped into her dressing-gown, stealing down to the gallery. All was quiet, the hall lying still in the grey dawn light, but as Ilona approached Kyle's door she heard him muttering.

He seemed to be engaged in some feverish
dream, tossing beneath blankets that had slipped
from his bare arms and shoulders. Ilona caught
the words 'Hamish' and 'wouldn't' as she crept to
his bedside and bent to pull the covers more
securely round him.

'No, don't!' said Kyle more clearly, and opened
his eyes to look at her dazedly.

Worried to distraction, she laid a hand to his
forehead and found it alarmingly hot, though he
was shivering. His eyes stared at her fever-bright.

'I'm cold,' he muttered. 'Warm me.'

'Just lie still,' Ilona breathed. 'I'll get Mrs
McTavish.'

'No!' As she tried to move away his hand locked
round her wrist, dragging her back so that she fell
across the edge of the bed and was forced to sit
there. 'Warm me,' he said again.

'Kyle, please!'

With inhuman strength, he lifted her until she
lay half on top of him, then his hands caught her
face and pulled her down to meet the unnatural
heat of his lips. His arms clasped round her
immovably. He said hoarsely, 'I love you. Stay
with me.'

Unable to move, Ilona rested her head on his
naked breast and relaxed against him, fearing that
resistance would only increase his fevered determination. He didn't know what he was doing,
or saying, and obviously he had no idea who she
was. Most probably he had taken her for Morag.

'Stay!' he sighed, his arms tightening until she
could hardly breathe.

'All right!' she whispered. 'But don't hold me so
tight, Kyle. You're hurting me.'

'Don't say that!' Rough fingers sought her chin,

lifting it. He searched her face with glazed eyes and rolled over with her, kissing her passionately in a way that made her senses swoop despite the heat radiating from him and the fact that she knew he was delirious.

One sweep of his arm drew the blankets to cover her, his naked body like fire through her night-clothes, and her hands, of their own accord, began to stroke the muscles of his back as her lips parted in response to his demands. Then with a sigh he laid his head on her shoulder, wrapping himself around her, and she felt him relax into sleep.

Ilona must have slept, too, for she came awake to find herself streaming with sweat induced by the fever in Kyle's body. Gently twisting her head to look at his face she saw that his hair was damp, his skin glistening. The fever had broken and he was deeply asleep, worn out by his tossing and turning.

When she lifted herself on to one elbow his arms fell limply from around her and she carefully slid out of the bed, watching his face. Her movements had not disturbed him, she was glad to see.

'Oh, Kyle!' she breathed, tenderly kissing his unresponsive lips and stroking his sweat-damp hair. 'If only you meant it!'

Tears stung her eyes as she made sure the blankets covered him properly. How ill he looked, so weak and helpless that she was deathly afraid. Not knowing what else to do, she ran to rouse Mrs McTavish, who at once took charge and dispatched Ilona to make herself some coffee.

From the basement kitchen she watched the sun lift above the hills to pour its golden light on to the lochside, but that morning the beauty of Drumm had little power to stir her. Suppose Kyle didn't recover? What would she do without him? What would Drumm do?

Restless, she went out and wandered among the flowers in the sloping garden. There below, on the edge of the loch, the single huge boulder lay touched to gold by the first edge of sunlight. Mairi's rock, Ilona thought, where the poor island girl had sat wishing for Magnus Bright Axe to come back to her. But this time there was a twist in the story. This time it was the mermaid who had fallen in love with the Viking prince.

Sitting on a stone seat in a blossom-covered arbour, she laid her head in her hands and wept as she at last admitted to her own feelings. She was no longer puzzled by the conflicting mixture of her own emotions; she knew what was causing it. She loved Kyle Lachlan with all her heart and soul, Drumm or no Drumm, oil or no oil. It wasn't logical, but she could no longer lie to herself. She loved him, and if anything happened to him then her life would be one long regret.

CHAPTER NINE

'WISHT, lassie,' said Mrs McTavish, bustling out to
find her, 'do you want to make yourself ill, sitting
on that cold stone in your dressing-gown? Come
away in and have some breakfast. And don't weep
any more. He's strong. It will take more than a
wee fever to take Mr Kyle away from us, never
you fret. Why, when he wakes in a few hours he'll
be wanting his food, and in a day or two he'll be
up and ordering us both around, like always.'

'But it was my fault!' Ilona cried. 'That's the
third time he's got soaked because of me. If I
hadn't told Hugh to come back, Kyle might not be
ill now.'

'Och, we can none of us see what lies ahead. We
can only do what seems right at the time. What's
the point of blaming yourself? Dry your eyes, now.
When he wakes he'll want to see you, I dare say,
and you don't want your face to be all pink and
puffy, now do you?'

'No, I suppose not,' Ilona sighed, though she
didn't think Kyle would have any particular wish
to see her, nor did she relish the thought of having
to visit the sickroom and pretend that she didn't
want him with every nerve and sinew in her body.

A quick shower made her feel slightly better,
then wearing a cotton shirt and blue jeans she ate
breakfast in the morning room, which was set in a
turret corner of the castle with leaded windows
looking across the hillside. From that vantage
point she saw Jock McIver walking round towards

151

the back door, with his faithful collie leaping round his heels.

'A letter for you,' Mrs McTavish announced when she came in a few minutes later. 'Mr McIver brought it. It came with the provision boat this morning.'

With a slight grimace of chagrin, Ilona recognised her aunt's handwriting.

'Your letters are so few and far between,' Zoe South had written, even her writing managing to convey the complaining whine which so irritated Ilona. 'It's really very naughty of you when you know I'm eager to know every last detail. However, I've decided to take a little break and come and see for myself how you're doing up there in the wilds. The trains are frightfully expensive, but I expect I can manage the fare. I'll be arriving on Thursday at two-forty-five, always assuming that British Rail will run on time for once. I'm sure you can arrange to meet me and see me safely across to the island. Marianne sends her love. All news when I see you. Yours affectionately, Aunt Zoe.'

How very like Aunt Zoe to invite herself, Ilona thought with exasperation. What was she coming for—to inspect the island and the castle and turn up her nose at everything? For two pins Ilona would have sent a telegram to put her aunt off—she might say that everyone on Drumm had suddenly contracted some contagious disease. But no, that would never do. Aunt Zoe would have to be allowed to come. Ilona supposed that her aunt did have a certain right to see the island.

One thing she was sure of—after the fiasco of Hugh's unexpected arrival she would not risk angering Kyle by having another stranger turn up without his prior knowledge. He must be told that Zoe South was about to descend on his island refuge.

Since Mrs McTavish had told her that Kyle was awake, she trailed up the stairs with the letter in one hand, hoping that he wouldn't remember their encounter of the early hours. She was unwilling to face him, but knew she could not put off a meeting for long.

'Come in,' his voice replied to her knock.

She opened the door, but remained on the threshold, glad to see that he looked better, if not entirely well. For one thing he wasn't so flushed, but there were hollows round his eyes and his face seemed more craggy than normal. He sat leaning against pillows, his upper body berry-brown beside the white linen, and his expression was one of polite indifference beneath an uncombed mop of red curls.

'How are you feeling?' Ilona asked.

'I'm all right,' he replied. 'For heaven's sake, come in—I won't bite. Leaving the door open makes a horrible draught in here.'

Ilona closed the door, though she stayed by it for fear that if she went nearer to Kyle she might go all the way and throw herself into his arms. 'You ought to be wearing pyjamas,' she said.

'I don't possess any,' he replied. 'Anyway, I'm warm enough. I just don't want to be in a draught. What's the weather like?'

'Very summery.'

'Lucky for you. If you'd arrived in autumn, with the winter to follow, it might have been a different story. But I suppose come October you'll be off with Hugh Danvers, so you'll never see Drumm at its worst.'

Ilona opened her mouth to deny having any intention of going away with Hugh, but what was the use? If Kyle thought she was involved with Hugh that would prevent him from guessing her real feelings and having a good laugh at her expense.

'You're probably right,' she said, not looking at him. 'But you'll have Morag to keep you warm.'

She chanced a glance at his unreadable face. No, he didn't remember dragging her into bed with him to 'warm him.' Thank heaven for that.

'Anyway, I came to show you this letter,' she added. 'It's from my aunt.'

He held out his hand. 'Bring it here.'

Hesitating for a second, Ilona walked across the room, just far enough to be able to hand him the letter at arm's length. Kyle gave her a mirthless smile and began to read.

'All your friends and relatives seem to assume they have the right to descend on us uninvited,' he said with a frown. 'I hope we're not going to spend the summer providing cheap holidays, especially if they're all like this. She sounds a real dragon.'

'She's not really so bad,' Ilona said swiftly. 'May I take it you don't mind? I could always phone and put her off.'

He waved a weary hand. 'Oh, let her come. Let them all come. Go and see Mike Nevis—the writer bloke I told you about, He's got a cabin cruiser and if you ask him nicely he'll take you across to meet your aunt. He owes me a favour.'

'I appreciate your co-operation, Kyle,' she said, meaning it.

Giving her a bleak glance, he tossed her the letter and slid down further into the bed. 'Put it down to illness. I haven't the strength to argue. And close the door behind you, please.'

On the specified day, Ilona cruised with Mike Nevis to the mainland and met her aunt at the station. Zoe South said she was 'absolutely shattered' after the long train journey and the thought of a sea voyage turned her stomach, but on meeting Mike Nevis she brightened, since he was so charming with her. Ilona only hoped that Kyle would be equally pleasant.

During the trip, Aunt Zoe exclaimed at the views of the sea, with the islands set like emeralds in azure. She was seeing the Western Isles at their best, Ilona thought. If it had been stormy, Aunt Zoe might have turned green.

'Oh!' her aunt exclaimed as they curved round the point and entered the sea-loch, coming within sight of the ancient grey house set above its gardens. 'Oh, Ilona, you naughty girl, you didn't tell me it was paradise! Marianne will love it. She and her family hope to visit you later this year.'

Oh lord, Ilona sighed to herself. Kyle had been right.

Mrs McTavish was on the shore to greet them and help carry the luggage. They climbed the stepped pathways as the cruiser moved away, heading back to the harbour.

'Mr Lachlan said he'd get up,' Mrs McTavish told Ilona, who didn't know whether to be pleased or sorry.

'Is he well enough?' she asked.

'He says so, and you know what he's like—pigheaded as a mule.'

Aunt Zoe laughed. 'Surely only a pig can be pigheaded, Mrs McTavish. I fancy you're mixing your metaphors. But don't worry. If Mr Lachlan isn't feeling up to par I shall soon make him go back to bed. I never yet met the man I couldn't handle.'

Behind her back, Ilona exchanged a speaking glance with the housekeeper. Her aunt was tempting fate, because she had yet to meet Kyle Lachlan.

As they went into the hall, Kyle himself rose from an armchair by the fireplace, slowly unfolding his six foot three. He was still a little pale beneath his tan, but otherwise the fever had left him unmarked and as he straightened a shaft of sunlight through a high window caught in his hair, turning it red as flame. Against his black shirt and cords the effect was startling, and Aunt Zoe came to a full stop.

'I'll take the cases up,' said Mrs McTavish, relieving Ilona of her burden.

'Good heavens!' Aunt Zoe muttered under her breath. 'Is that . . .?'

'Yes, it is,' Ilona replied, allowing herself to rejoice in Kyle's magnificence, but only momentarily. She had no right to be proud of him, she reminded herself, but oh, how fine he looked. He was probably the most beautiful man in the world.

'Kyle,' she said aloud, 'I'd like you to meet my aunt Zoe—Mrs South.'

He strolled across the big room, extending a hand. 'My pleasure, Mrs South. South . . . I seem to have heard that name before.' A sidelong glance sardonically reminded Ilona of her deception when she first arrived, and she felt herself redden.

'I expect Ilona mentioned it,' said Aunt Zoe.

'Yes,' with another flick of mocking grey at Ilona, 'I expect that must be it. Won't you come and sit down? Mrs McTavish will be bringing tea in a few minutes.'

'Thank you, but I think I'd like to freshen up first, if you'll excuse me. Which way is my room, Ilona? You'll come with me, of course.'

'Of course,' said Ilona, only too glad to escape when Kyle was in that dangerously tame mood.

Aware that he was watching, she led the way upstairs and into the guest room, where Mrs McTavish was turning down the bed.

'That will be all, thank you,' Aunt Zoe said imperiously, and Mrs McTavish departed, bristling.

'She's not a servant, Aunt Zoe,' Ilona protested. 'She's more like family.'

'Whose family?' her aunt demanded, removing her hat and fussing with her tightly-permed hair. 'That man's? Really, Ilona, I can see I haven't come before time. You failed to tell me he was so ... so ... so male!'

'What did you think he was—android?' Ilona retorted.

Her aunt gave her a severe look. 'Don't use that tone with me, young lady. You know very well you gave me the impression he was much older. Just what has been going on here? I trust you haven't joined the permissive society!'

Two months before, Ilona would have backed down, but she had enjoyed a taste of independence and now she looked her aunt in the eye.

'I believe I'm old enough to know what I'm doing, Aunt Zoe.'

'I knew it!' her aunt cried. 'You've forgotten everything I taught you. I could sense the vibrations downstairs. A man like that ... Men are not to be trusted; I've learned that through bitter experience. And where's Hugh? Discarded, I suppose, for that . . . that redheaded Titan!'

Ilona moved towards the door, furious with her aunt's assessment of her character, and Kyle's. 'The main bathroom's next door,' she said. 'I'll see you in the hall for tea in five minutes.'

The three of them managed to take tea with awkward politeness, though Kyle continued to give Ilona veiled looks that convinced her he was having trouble maintaining his manners. It was a relief when he left them to take a stroll in the garden, and Aunt Zoe declared she had a headache and would lie down for a while before dinner. Ilona, too, sought her tower room, where she spent the next hour or so wishing her aunt back in Surrey as she peered from the window for a glimpse of Kyle's red head among the trees below.

In a mist of perfume, she slid into her shell-pink dress preparing for dinner, only to discover a small stain on the skirt. Aunt Zoe's sharp, critical eyes would notice that at once. She opened her wardrobe and frowned over her choice—the primrose cotton, which was demure, or the new, expensive black, which most definitely was not. To please Aunt Zoe, or to outrage? Ilona opted for cowardice and safety.

As she descended the stairs she saw Kyle watching from the hall below, dressed formally but conventionally.

'Scared to wear your new black dress?' he murmured as she approached.

Ilona tilted her chin. 'Scared to wear the kilt?' she replied, and was disconcerted when the challenge in his eyes became a twinkle, telling her that he, too, had considered her aunt's sensibilities.

Aunt Zoe appeared, cool in a classic linen shirtwaister, and Kyle offered drinks. Eventually they moved into the dining hall, whose splendours made Aunt Zoe exclaim with pleasure as she mentally priced each item on view, making Ilona feel uncomfortable.

'I had no idea it would be like this,' her aunt said at length, after several glasses of wine. 'But now that I've seen it I know exactly what I shall do. I'll sell the lodge—it's so expensive to run just for one. Then I can come and keep you company, Ilona.'

Ilona nearly choked on her food. A glance at Kyle confirmed that he was equally astounded, and not at all pleased.

'You might not find it entirely congenial as a permanent home,' he replied, 'even if I invited you to live here, which I don't recall doing.'

'But Ilona is my niece, practically my daughter!'

'You'd be so far from Marianne and the baby!' Ilona exclaimed. 'Oh, you wouldn't settle here, Aunt Zoe. What about all your friends, and the bridge club?'

'I expect I could soon make new friends,' her aunt said, her eyes hard. 'Mr Lachlan, you can surely understand why I cannot let Ilona remain here alone with you. It's not ... not quite the thing—the two of you alone here.'

'We're not alone,' Kyle told her. 'We have Mrs McTavish as a chaperone. I'm sorry, Mrs South, but your idea is out of the question. You're welcome to visit, of course, but——'

'This house,' Aunt Zoe said firmly, her mouth pursing into a mass of lines, 'belongs partly to Ilona. And since I brought her up I believe I'm entitled to some recompense in my declining years.'

At this, Kyle rose from his chair, towering over the table with a face darkened by angry blood, his eyes like cold steel. 'I believe you have a daughter of your own. Get your pound of flesh from her, Mrs South. And let me remind you that Ilona has nothing—not until she has been here for six months.'

Aunt Zoe had paled, but she wasn't entirely cowed. 'I shudder to think what might happen in that length of time. It's not decent! Ilona is a defenceless girl, and you——'

'And I'm a filthy lecher, I suppose,' Kyle said coldly. 'Thank you for that snap judgment, Mrs South. But if that's all that's keeping you here, let me put your mind at rest. I'd be quite happy to marry Ilona any time she chooses. Excuse me.'

In the silence that followed his departure, Ilona felt sick. Her aunt appeared to have lost her tongue, but after a while she turned to Ilona with a triumphant smile.

'You see! You have to know how to handle men. You'll accept, of course—well, naturally you will. You'd be a fool not to, when all of this goes with him.'

Distressed beyond bearing, Ilona pushed back her chair, said, 'Oh, Aunt Zoe, how can you be so mercenary?' and fled.

Entering the breakfast room the next morning, Ilona was dismayed to find Kyle there at the table reading a day-old paper. He glanced up briefly, but if he noticed her pallor he made no comment, only nodded, 'Morning.'

'Good morning,' Ilona replied. 'I didn't expect . . . How do you feel this morning?'

'I feel fine,' he said from behind his paper. 'I had a good early night, didn't I?'

She helped herself to coffee and toast and sat down opposite him. 'I should have known better than to let Aunt Zoe come.'

'On the contrary, it's been quite an experience meeting her. From odd things you've said I'd gained an impression which she only confirmed last night. One thing's certain—she isn't coming to live here. Did she approve of my proposal?'

Faced with a wall of newsprint, Ilona bit her lip miserably. 'Yes, she did. But *I* didn't. How could you say such a thing? What about Morag?'

'What about her?'

'You're supposed to be marrying her!'

The paper rustled and for a moment she was afforded a glimpse of his red hair and cool grey eyes before the barrier went up again. 'What gave you that impression?'

'She did! You must have led her to believe . . .' His distant disdain infuriated her and she reached out to tear the paper from his hands, throwing it to the floor. 'You don't seriously expect me to marry you just to get rid of Aunt Zoe?'

'Not solely for that, no,' he said with a shrug. 'But as I've said before, it would make things a good deal simpler. This island has to be run as a single unit. It can't be split into two halves. If we were married . . .'

'For convenience, you mean?' Ilona choked.

'Of course. What else is there?'

'Shouldn't there be love?' she protested. 'Doesn't that enter into your calculations at all?'

He lifted a surprised eyebrow. 'Love? You can get all you need of that from Hugh Danvers. Since he's so obsessed with long barrows there are several on other islands, which should keep him busy for quite some time—and conveniently on hand. I wouldn't object to that.'

'And I suppose you'd go off seeing Morag any time you pleased!'

'Well, naturally. Faithfulness is an outdated concept, isn't it?'

'Oh, you——' Unable to stop herself, Ilona threw her coffee over him, though luckily it was fairly cool. Watching it drip down his stony face she stood shaking, knowing she had gone too far. She turned to make a rush for the door, but with athletic ease Kyle got there before her and laid his hands on her shoulders, shaking her violently.

When the motion stopped, Ilona stared at him, breathless, seeing the fury in his eyes.

'Of course,' he said in a hoarse, throaty voice, 'I wouldn't let our marriage go unconsummated. I'd expect you to cater to my needs.'

He dropped his head and kissed her brutally. Ilona squirmed, sickened by what was happening, her fists clenched tightly against his chest in a hopeless effort to get away, but he only slid his arms firmly round her, pressing her close to his body, while his lips moved down to her throat to rest on the pulse that jumped erratically there.

Ilona felt her mind spinning, caught in the whirlpool of her love for him. But it couldn't be love, since she hated him. It must be pure physical reaction. The thought nauseated her and with a superhuman effort she twisted out of his arms.

'You must be mad if you think I'd marry you!' she spat at him. 'You're nothing but a heartless, brutal . . . I hate you, Kyle Lachlan! Hate you!'

A smile that was iceberg-cold twisted itself round his lips. 'Then why don't you pack your things and go home with your aunt, Miss McGregor?'

'I'll never leave! Do you think I'd leave Drumm in your clutches?'

'On the contrary, I'm quite sure you'll stay, if you can. Your aunt taught you well. The inheritance is a great deal of money, isn't it? Excuse me, I have work to do.'

With impotent anger, Ilona slapped the side of her fist against the wall as the door closed behind him. So he thought her a fortune-hunter, did he? Yet he was the one who wanted Drumm's riches for himself. He was just being as unbearable as possible in the hope of driving her away.

During the morning, a message came from Mrs McIver, who had been informed that Marianne had been rushed into hospital for an appendix operation. Ilona couldn't decide which was the stronger of her emotions—concern, or relief.

'I must go home,' her aunt said. 'They'll need someone to look after the baby. But I hate leaving you here, Ilona. Promise me you'll behave yourself. If you've really no intention of marrying that man, then please be careful. I've seen the way he looks at you.'

What way was that? Ilona wondered. Like a lustful, frustrated male animal?

'You needn't worry,' she said. 'I couldn't let a man near me unless I was in love with him, and Kyle isn't at all the type of man I could care for. Let me help you pack.'

She was thankful that her aunt didn't guess she was lying. Kyle was not the sort of man she had dreamed girlish dreams about, but then until now she hadn't known that men like Kyle existed. Only he had the power to stir her innermost feelings. One look at him and she felt weak, wanting him to hold her tenderly. But since tenderness was not in his nature she would have to live through this insane phase and just hope that some day soon she could view him dispassionately.

Kyle, called from his work to make yet another emergency flight, this time for Aunt Zoe's benefit, was polite and concerned, but Ilona knew that beneath his surface efficiency he was quietly pleased to be getting rid of his unwelcome visitor so soon after her arrival.

'I'll come again as soon as Marianne is perfectly recovered,' Aunt Zoe promised as she boarded the helicopter. Or was it a threat?

Unable to settle to anything, Ilona walked down to the village, the June breeze flirting with her light cotton skirt. But her face was abstracted as she wrestled mentally with her problems. As Kyle took pleasure in reminding her, she had no rights on Drumm as yet. Could she endure the rest of the summer in his company, loving him and hating him as she did? Her own feelings bewildered her. At times she remembered his infrequent softer moods and told herself that she must have been mistaken about him; then she recalled how he had tried to keep her away, and then attempted to drive her from the island. He didn't want her on Drumm, and his reason seemed clear—it was plain greed.

Old Alice McVeigh leaned on her gate, her black eyes narrowed as she watched Ilona approach, slender in the sunlight with her long hair blowing round her shoulders.

'Good morning,' Ilona greeted her.

'Aye, it is,' the old woman agreed. 'Your aunt's gone, then? Her daughter took sick.'

'News does get around, doesn't it?' Ilona said drily.

'Aye, well, there's not much excitement on Drumm. But there's something in the wind. It's coming. Can't you smell it?' She lifted her face, wrinkling her brown nose as she breathed of the breeze. 'He'll be back, the dark-haired man.'

'I don't think so,' Ilona said. 'Mr Lachlan made it very clear he wasn't welcome.'

'Aye, so he did. But it's not over yet. You mark my words, he'll be back. And then Mr Lachlan had better watch himself.'

Disturbed by the certainty in the old woman's voice, Ilona said, 'I'm not sure what you mean. My friend Mr Danvers doesn't present a threat to Kyle.'

'Depends how you look at it,' Alice answered, wagging her head. 'I always knew there was fateful doings to come for Kyle Lachlan. I knew it, even when he was a wee lad.'

'You've known him all his life?' Ilona asked.

'I have. I knew his mother, too. And his father.'

Ilona's ears were all attuned now, wondering if she might learn the secret of the 'gossip'. 'His father?'

'Aye.' The old woman peered myopically towards the harbour. 'Robert Lachlan was killed in a storm at sea and his wife left all alone wi' the bairn. So Hamish McGregor took them in. Some say Jinnie Lachlan was his mistress, though she was years younger than him, but however it was he raised the boy like his own. Ah, you should have seen them, the sturdy lad striding the hills beside Hamish, and Hamish that proud of him. Those two were close as that.' She held up two fingers twined together. 'They thought the same.

That's why Hamish sent the boy to school and then to college, to educate him for the care of Drumm. It was as good as having a son of his own to follow him.'

At last Ilona realised why Kyle felt so possessive about the island. 'As good as having a son,' Alice had said. Hamish had loved him, and the feeling had been mutual—Ilona recalled how Kyle had hardly been able to bring himself to talk about the old man's death.

'Then why,' she asked faintly, 'did my great-uncle even give me the chance to share the island?'

'Who knows?' the old woman shrugged, fixing her with an unblinking stare. 'Maybe he wanted McGregor blood to continue here.'

Ilona felt herself flush and turned away. 'Then I'm afraid he'll be disappointed.'

'Oh, aye,' Alice agreed in a sly, knowing tone. 'The mermaid didn't stay. And Magnus Bright Axe died.'

'We're not living a legend!' Ilona protested, her nerves on edge. 'Even if I do leave, Kyle will still be here.'

'Maybe so,' said Alice, shaking her head. 'And maybe not.'

Thoroughly unsettled now, Ilona returned to Creag Mhor and saw the helicopter arrive. But though she waited for Kyle to call in at the house he did not come and she had to eat lunch alone, as she had done so often. Before the day was over, she promised herself, she would have things out with Kyle once and for all.

The day grew hotter. Wanting to cool her overworked brain, Ilona put on a bikini and robe and went down through the gardens to the lochside, where some of Hamish's carefully-

nurtured trees grew in a natural arbour at the edge
of a stony beach. She stepped carefully into the
water, wading until she could swim and enjoying
the slight chill against her skin.

Although she was not a strong swimmer, she
paddled around for a while before hauling herself
up on to Mairi's Rock to dry in the sun. Head
thrown back, her long hair hanging behind her,
she braced her arms against the rock and offered
herself to the warmth, slender limbs and body
revealed in all their curvaceous glory except for the
small barrier of the bikini.

Not far away, something splashed, and Ilona
looked round to see a swimmer, his body made
wavery by refraction, coming underwater towards
her from the lochside. He swam like a seal, with
such ease and strength that she knew who it must
be.

Kyle surfaced only a few feet away, his tanned
frame lifting dripping from the water as he threw
back his hair and rubbed his face. Water ran down
his bronzed body, across broad chest and flat
stomach, rivulets trickling down long, muscular
legs knee-deep in the sea. His only garment was
a minuscule pair of white trunks. Feeling the
now familiar stir inside her, Ilona sat forward, her
arms flung round her knees as if she could control
her body by that means, or hide it from his bold
gaze.

Having wiped the salt water from his face, Kyle
stood regarding her without expression. 'You
really look like a mermaid, sitting on that rock,' he
told her.

'I wish people would forget that stupid legend,'
she said edgily, worried by the memory of her
conversation with Alice McVeigh. 'Should you be

getting yourself wet so soon after that chill? It was your getting soaked that caused it.'

'No, it wasn't. I'd felt off colour all day, though the ducking didn't help.' He lowered wet-lashed eyes as if the memory still embarrassed him.

'I was in the village earlier,' Ilona told him, 'and I met Alice McVeigh. Why didn't you tell me the full truth about your relationship with Hamish? You were virtually his adopted son.'

'I didn't think it was relevant,' he said, and with one lithe movement jumped up to sit on the rock beside her, his arm brushing hers, causing a shock to jolt through her. 'Besides, I didn't want you to give up your claim out of charity.'

'But if I'd known . . .' she said unsteadily, her voice evidence that all her senses were jumping.

His eyes met hers, his face bare inches away, with a trickle of water running near his ear from hair turned mahogany by its wetness. Ilona started to turn away, but his hand against her cheek prevented her. 'If you'd known, what would you have done?'

Swallowing hard, she said, 'I might have understood you better. We needn't have been so much at loggerheads.'

'Maybe I enjoy arguing with you,' he said in an undertone. His thumb brushed her lips, his gaze following the motion, and fearing that he might see the way her mouth softened in response Ilona pushed his hand away, only to have him lay hold of her and press her back against the flat hardness of the rock, from where the sun behind him turned his hair into a flaming halo.

'Ilona!' he murmured in a vibrant voice, and bent to taste that tremulous mouth with a tenderness that astounded and delighted her, making her be still.

When he lifted his head, she stared up at him dazedly. 'You do care about Drumm, don't you? You won't ruin it just for a drop of oil?'

'Oil?' he said as if he had never heard the word.

Irritated, Ilona pushed him away, forced to endure the heady contact with his naked flesh before she could scramble clear and perch on the very edge of the rock away from him. 'Don't pretend any more, please! I saw the report. There's oil here, and you want it. You don't care what you do to get it.'

His face contorted with fury and a hand shot out to grasp her elbow. 'You've been spying!'

Trying to escape, Ilona half slid off the rock, scraping her shin painfully, but Kyle followed, into knee-deep water, roughly forcing her to wade ashore and up the pathways.

'Where are you taking me?' she demanded, but a black look was the only reply. 'Kyle!' The hand around her arm locked immovably and she was obliged to go where he took her, up to Creag Mhor, across the hall and into his study, where he all but threw her into a chair.

'Stay there!' he ordered, going to feel under the desk for a key which he used to unlock the file drawer. Out came the blue 'Reports' folder, tossed on to the desk. He riffled through it, extracting a sheet.

'Is this the report you saw? It's the only one that makes any mention of oil. Read it, Ilona.'

Trembling with rage at his manhandling of her, Ilona took the paper and read: 'Oil-bearing deposits.' There, she knew she had not been mistaken.

'Read it!' Kyle grated when she glanced up. 'All of it.'

Ilona did so. The stiff, jargon-filled phrases were difficult to follow, but as she frowned at the page it began to dawn on her that she had misread it the first time. It was true that the tests had revealed the presence of oil, but the report's conclusion decided that it was such a small field as to be financially worthless of exploitation.

There would be no oil from Drumm.

Her face burned as the paper trembled in her hand. She daren't look at Kyle; she was too ashamed of the dreadful things she had thought about him.

'At least now I understand some of the things you've said,' he told her, his voice thick with disgust. 'And the questions you asked Mr McKay. But I'm afraid a half-share of the income won't be as much as you imagined, since there is no oil. You and Danvers will have to manage without it.'

Ilona did look up then, tears dazzling her sight. 'Kyle . . .' she croaked. How out of place he looked, a naked savage in office surroundings, his face cold with contempt.

'No, don't say anything,' his voice came harsh through her misery. 'It's too late for that. What has become clear is that we can't possibly continue the way we are. Since you don't trust me, you'll have to find yourself a new factor.'

She jumped to her feet, hands out in appeal. 'Nobody else could do the job the way you do!' she choked in dismay. 'You love this island.'

'I did.' His tone was gruff, but firm with decision. 'You've poisoned it for me, though. I shall leave, Ilona. And that's my final word.'

CHAPTER TEN

FOR the first time, Ilona felt herself truly an alien on Drumm. She saw little of Kyle, who went out with the dawn and returned with the sunset, which was very late in the evening since they were near midsummer. He ate in the kitchen with Mrs McTavish and when he did happen to meet Ilona he would not talk to her beyond the briefest politenesses. His mind was made up. He intended to leave as soon as he had tied up a few ends. Even Mrs McTavish, sensing the atmosphere, found excuses to avoid Ilona, and if Ilona went to the village she was met with hostile stares and tight-closed lips.

But Kyle couldn't leave! she kept thinking. He wouldn't actually walk out and leave no one to supervise affairs on the island. She could not believe that he meant it. But as several days passed there seemed no weakening in his determination. He was really intending to go—because he couldn't stand being anywhere near her.

One morning as she went down the stairs she found him waiting for her in the hall, as remote and hard as the mainland mountains.

'I just thought I should tell you that I shall be away for a few days,' he announced. 'There's a man I have to see—about the factor's job. He's a friend of mine, highly qualified and experienced, and I've suggested it might be an idea for him to come as my replacement. If it works out, I'll ask him to present himself for an interview at Creag

Mhor. Presumably you'd like a final say in the appointment.'

Ilona listened in disbelief, all colour draining from her face. 'We don't need another factor!' she gasped. 'No one knows Drumm the way you do. You can't be serious. You can't just hand the place over to a stranger.'

'I can if I think he can handle it,' he said, and strode out without more ado.

Shivering despite the warmth of the day, Ilona sat down on the bottom stair, her legs no longer able to support her. Until that moment she hadn't entirely believed that he would do it, but now she was convinced. She felt sick when she realised it was all because of her. She had made him hate the island, his own home, where he had grown up, where his life was.

What could she do to stop him? He wouldn't listen to apologies and he was impervious to reason. Perhaps if she promised never to meddle again ... But that wouldn't make any difference, she knew. He had once accused her of lousing up his life just by coming to Drumm, and events appeared to have proved him all too right.

Suddenly Ilona knew that she couldn't allow him to leave. Which left only one alternative— since she was the outsider, the usurper, she must be the one to go.

Hoping to catch him before he took off, she ran out of the house, only to see the helicopter lifting to soar over the castle. But perhaps it was as well. She didn't fancy more arguments. Her road lay clear before her and she could be gone within twenty-four hours if she made haste. She shaded her eyes to watch the machine dwindle in the distance.

'Goodbye, Kyle,' she whispered to the breeze that cooled the tears on her face. She would never see him again, and the knowledge caused a heavy pain in her heart. If only things had been different! If only she hadn't been so headstrong and reckless. But she was as she was, and all she could do now was leave as swiftly as possible so that Kyle, and Drumm, could recover from the upheaval of her coming.

Going down to the village, she asked to use the radio-phone and called Hugh Danvers at the inn on the mainland.

'Hugh? How are you?'

'Better for hearing your voice,' he replied. 'I'm fine, apart from this plaster on my arm. When are you coming to see me?'

'Soon, Hugh. Listen, will you do something for me? I want you to ask Donald Ogg to come and fetch me. Tomorrow, if that's possible. Tell him to come to the shore below the castle—it's all right, Kyle's away for a few days, and anyway it doesn't matter since I'm officially asking Donald to come. I'll watch out for him, and meet him when I see the boat. I just want him to take me to the mainland. Have you got that?'

'Yes, of course,' said Hugh. 'But what's the . . .'

'Just do it, Hugh,' she replied, and broke the connection. She felt calmer now, though it was the cold, empty calm that came with total despair.

That night she tried to write a letter to Kyle, giving up all claim to the island and asking his forgiveness for the wrong she had done him. She wrote that she loved him too much to see him leave his home because of her.

And then she screwed the letter up tightly and tossed it into the waste-paper basket, berating herself. Words were inadequate. He would never forgive her, and why should she admit to her love for him? He had never wanted her on Drumm, and if he had felt anything for her it had been only desire prompted by lack of other women. From the moment they met he had behaved badly towards her, and to know she had fallen in love with him would probably cause him great amusement.

When dawn came, she packed her cases and took them down to the hall, much to Mrs McTavish's displeasure.

'So you're running away,' the housekeeper sniffed. 'I thought you had more grit in your craw than that.'

'Would you rather see Kyle leave?' Ilona asked miserably. 'That's the choice you have—him or me.'

'I'd rather see you both stay and stop being such blethering idiots!' Mrs McTavish chafed. 'Wisht, what a couple of ninnies you are! But don't let me interfere. What am I to tell him when he comes home?'

'Just tell him . . . tell him I'm sorry and I'll never bother him again, in any way.'

The housekeeper shook her head impatiently and went on her way.

Ilona spent the morning taking a last slow look around Creag Mhor, trying to imprint it on her mind to take back to Surrey with her. All too clearly now, she saw that she should never have come to Drumm. She had been prompted by a longing for adventure that somehow seemed childish now. Well, she must pay for it by going home to face Aunt Zoe's scorn, which would make life at the lodge even more uncomfortable than it had been before. Worst of all was the knowledge that she had hurt Kyle, and as a result she must live without him. Oh yes, fate had designed a fine punishment for her foolish impetuosity.

Unable to be still, she wandered out by the front door intending to walk quietly round the gardens one last time, bidding goodbye to the trees, flowers, and the screaming gulls of Drumm. But as she emerged from the house a slender figure came down the last slope from the village—Morag Frazer, with the blazing eyes of a Valkyrie.

'Just what do you think you're playing at?' Morag demanded. 'I saw Kyle last night, and he says he's leaving Drumm. Well, let me tell you, Miss Ilona McGregor, that before I'll let him throw away what is rightfully his I'll scratch your eyes out. *You're* the one who doesn't belong here. Kyle's worked all his life for this rotten island. If anyone deserves the rewards it's him, not you— not a little nobody who never set foot here until she saw a fortune in it!'

'Isn't that what you see in it, too?' Ilona asked dully. 'You think you can persuade Kyle to sell Drumm, but I don't believe he ever will. Not for you. Not for anyone.'

'He would sell it if it all belonged to him!' Morag exclaimed. 'As it is, you can prevent him from disposing of his half. He'll have nothing! He's such a fool he won't even claim half the profits, since the island will need his share, too, just to keep going. Haven't you got any shame? You're as bad as a thief! Why did you ever come here interfering?'

'I've been asking myself that for days now,' said Ilona.

Opening her mouth to pour more vitriol, Morag

paused and gaped as if she didn't believe her ears.
'You've what?'

'I believe you heard what I said. You've had a
wasted journey, Morag. I'm the one who's leaving.
Kyle will be sole owner of Drumm. But you've
misjudged him if you think he'll sell it. He loves it
here. He won't leave.'

Morag's eyes narrowed. She looked Ilona up
and down, noting her cheap cotton shirt and worn
jeans. 'We shall see about that after you've gone,
Miss Mouse. Without your presence to unsettle
him, he'll see it my way sooner or later. Whatever
he may have said, he was never in love with you. It
was just proximity making him behave like a
moonstruck schoolboy.'

Puzzled, Ilona said, 'I don't know what you
mean. I never thought he was in love with me.'

'You mean he didn't——' False eyelashes batted
furiously over eyes that flickered with racing
thoughts. 'Well, no, you had no reason to believe
that, I suppose, but you might have harboured
romantic dreams. He *is* a very attractive man.'

What on earth had she stopped herself from
blurting out? Had Kyle said something to make
Morag think he was in love with Ilona? No, that
wasn't possible, because it wasn't true. But before
she could figure it all out logically she glanced at
the loch and saw a dinghy rounding the point.

It was time to leave.

'Here's Donald Ogg,' she said, almost to herself.
'I must take my cases down to the landing point.
I'll just say goodbye to Mrs McTavish.'

Turning blindly, she went into the house and
ran down to the basement kitchen.

'I must go, Mrs McTavish. Donald Ogg is
coming.'

'Aye,' was all the housekeeper said, in such doom-laden tones that Ilona felt a chill run through her.

'Well ... goodbye. And thank you. I'm sorry . . .' Her voice choked off.

'Och, lassie!' Mrs McTavish got out, and suddenly threw her arms around Ilona, enveloping her in a brief bear-hug as she planted a smacking kiss on her cheek. 'We'll miss you. We'll miss you sorely.'

'And I'll miss you,' said Ilona, turning to run back up to the hall before she broke down and wept.

Morag was waiting, already carrying one of the cases and clearly enjoying the prospect of helping Ilona to leave Drumm. With a composure that was only on the surface, Ilona followed the dark-haired girl down the stepped paths through the lovely gardens. The dinghy was well into the loch by that time, its sail bellying in the breeze, and to Ilona's surprise she saw that there were two men in it— Hugh had come with Donald Ogg. It seemed portentous, and her scalp prickled as she remembered the legend.

To allow for easy access to the boat, she stood on the ledge of rock at one side of the beach, where several feet of water lapped below her. Despite herself, she recalled the day when Kyle had dived from this spot and swum underwater to Mairi's rock, where he had kissed her with such tenderness. Had she misunderstood his moods after all? But it was too late to back out of what she had planned.

Glancing at Morag's satisfied smirk, Ilona thought crazily that the scene was now set—the dark-haired man was coming to fetch the

mermaid, who had left Creag Mhor with the aid of
the girl who loved the Viking. All it needed now
was for the helicopter to arrive, as Magnus Bright
Axe's ship had arrived . . . No! She shook herself
angrily, trying to rid her mind of the fey thoughts.
She was no mermaid and this was not the Dark
Ages. History did not repeat itself, not in that way.

Every muscle tensed against the storm of tears
that tore inside her, she watched the dinghy's sail
come down as Donald Ogg released the ropes and
Hugh, holding the tiller with his good arm,
brought the boat in close to the ledge.

'I don't know what this is all about,' said Hugh,
'but I assume you want to be away at once?'

'As soon as possible,' Ilona told him, handing
Donald one case, then the second, before pausing
to look at Morag, who smiled triumphantly and
backed away, saying, 'Goodbye—and good rid-
dance.'

'You're sure about this, are you?' asked Hugh.

'Perfectly sure.' Reaching for Donald's helping
hand, she stepped into the swaying boat, and at
that precise moment the helicopter shot over the
hill and settled towards its pad. Ilona sat down
heavily, feeling that she was trapped in a bad
dream, her thoughts all mixed up with horrifying
memories of the legend. 'Hurry. Hurry, please,'
she urged.

With practised movements, Donald hoisted his
sail, secured it and took over the tiller, saying that
he would have to tack against the wind to get back
down the loch. Ilona watched the hillside, wanting
to scream for speed, wanting to be away before
Kyle could come, as with maddening slowness the
boat moved out into open water, away from
Mairi's rock.

Tears glazed her eyes as she saw Creag Mhor clearly again, proud and grey above its bright gardens against the backdrop of the cliff. She wanted to look away, but something prevented her. This was her last look at the place she had come to love—the first place which had really felt like home to her.

She fancied she heard Mrs McTavish's voice raised, then a movement among the trees drew her eyes to where Kyle was plunging down the path, taking the steps two at a time. Morag's slim figure went to meet him, almost a hundred yards away now, dwindling as the boat gathered speed. Kyle erupted on to the beach and Morag threw out her hands, obviously attempting to prevent whatever he had in mind, but he brushed her aside and ran on, straight into the water.

Then the boom swept round and the boat veered, making a direct line for the open sea. The white sail dazzled her eyes, preventing her from seeing the tiny figures on the shore, but she heard Kyle's voice, lifted above the wind, ricocheting round the hills in a pain-filled howl. 'Ilona! Ilona-a-a!!'

They were rounding the point, the crag shutting off any possibility of another glance of Creag Mhor. Ilona felt unnaturally calm, her ears still ringing to the awful sound of her name being yelled so forlornly, though she felt sure that the echo had added the note of deep melancholy. She stared at the steep green flank of the island, but all she could see was Kyle, as she had last seen him, thigh-deep in the loch with Morag standing behind him on Mairi's rock.

She turned unseeing eyes to Hugh, asking, 'Did he try to come after us? Did you see?'

'Lachlan?' he said. 'No, I don't think so. Ilona, are you all right? You look as if you'd seen a ghost. What's been happening?'

'She's mebbe thinking aboot the Viking,' Donald Ogg told him. 'Magnus Bright Axe. Och, dinna fash yoursel', Miss McGregor. Mr Lachlan wouldna be so daft.'

He was right, of course, Ilona thought. Kyle wouldn't be stupid enough to try swimming after the dinghy. Why on earth should he? Events had come uncannily close to matching the legend, but the feelings were all different.

Yet she couldn't forget that note of anguish in Kyle's voice as he had yelled her name. Wrapped in with her misery, she experienced a timeless, dreamlike numbness as the dinghy sailed its slow way across the Sound and Drumm gradually dropped away behind, fading in the slight mist which always gathered round the islands when the day was fine. 'If you can see the mainland clearly,' Kyle had once said, 'you can be sure there's rain on the way.' The memory hurt more than was logical and she laid her head in her hands, blinking away the stupid futile tears.

'Are you going to tell me what happened?' asked Hugh.

'Nothing happened,' she said, her voice echoing through the emptiness inside her. 'I'm just going home, that's all.'

'Home? You mean ... You're giving up the inheritance? Are you out of your mind?'

Ilona looked at him, seeing a stranger. She wondered how she could ever have thought she cared for him. His work was his passion and he had made use of her only to get near the long

barrow. Quite suddenly she realised she had no
feelings left for him.

'No, Hugh,' she said quietly, 'I'm not mad. I
believe I'm growing up at long last.'

He looked baffled, but he made no attempt to
ask more questions as the boat sailed on. Behind
them, the Isle of Drumm had become a misty blur
on the horizon, but Ilona watched it, unable to
look away. A dark speck seemed to hover over the
island and she blinked hard to get rid of the
illusion, but the speck grew, coming closer, and
her heart seemed to turn over as she recognised the
Drumm helicopter. The roar of its engine reached
her, growing louder as the machine swept over the
dinghy, its downdraught fluttering the sail and
Ilona's hair.

'What's the fool playing at?' Hugh muttered as
the helicopter circled and came back to over-fly
them again, not quite low enough to interfere with
the progress of the boat, but still close enough to
make its presence felt. All the way back to the
mainland the helicopter stayed with them, swooping in figures of eight.

Avoiding the congestion of boats around the
harbour, Donald eased his dinghy in through the
mouth of the sea-loch, which indented the coast
like a fjord, and headed for the shelving ground
where Ilona had first met him. He was furling his
sail when the helicopter droned low overhead, its
draught rocking the dinghy before it passed and
flew to land on the bare green hilltop. Wondering
what Kyle meant to do, Ilona felt the boat bump
against the shore and Donald stepped out to
secure the rope, while on the hill not far away the
helicopter's rotors clattered to a stop and Kyle
jumped out.

'So what now?' Hugh asked as Ilona climbed unsteadily to dry land. 'Why has he come after you? I'm in no position to fight him off, not with my arm in a sling.'

Ilona hardly heard him. Her heart hammered in her throat as Kyle swung down the hill with jerky strides that told of his high temper even before she could clearly see that his face was grim as fate. He paused a few feet from her, his chest heaving beneath a half-open shirt, his hair tousled and his eyes flashing grey fire.

'Blast it, Ilona!' he exploded. 'Can't you ever do anything openly? You tried to sneak on to Drumm without my knowing, and now you'd leave the same way!'

Trembling, she lifted a hand to contain her blowing hair. 'I thought it was for the best. Drumm is yours, Kyle. I have no right to any part of it.'

He reached inside his pocket and took out a crumpled piece of paper which he waved at her angrily. It was the letter she had tried to write— the letter which said everything in her heart. She was so dismayed to see it in his hand that she could think of nothing to say as the colour rose in her cheeks.

'Just tell me one thing,' Kyle said roughly. 'Is it true, what you wrote in this letter? Is that why you're running away?'

Mutely miserable, she stood shaking, a tear dripping down her face.

Kyle swore deeply and eloquently, his voice hoarse. 'Good grief, girl, if I'd known that . . .' and before she guessed his intentions he swooped on her, sweeping her legs from beneath her so that she fell into his arms as he hoisted her into the air. Instinctively, she laced her hands behind his neck, struggling with a sense of unreality.

Dazed as she was, she saw Hugh and Donald both step forward as if to intervene, but they were stopped by a livid glance from Kyle. 'Away with you!' he roared. 'The lassie's mine!' and he turned on his heel to stride back up the hill, carrying Ilona as easily as if she were five years old.

'Kyle!' she breathed. It was meant to be a protest, but it came out on a choked, disbelieving laugh.

He stopped walking and looked into her eyes, his own gaze fierce with possessive passion. 'The Vikings knew a thing or two when it came to handling women. Sometimes brute force is the only answer. I certainly wasn't about to drown myself, not when I had the helicopter handy—not when I'd seen that letter. What the hell were you playing at, running out on me like that? I love you, woman. Didn't you know?'

At last she began to believe that she wasn't dreaming. Her fingers feathered through his hair as she studied his craggy face and those grey eyes that were bright with pain and love. Hardly knowing whether to laugh or cry, she said brokenly, 'How could I possibly know?'

'Women are supposed to know these things,' he said huskily. 'Female intuition, it's called. Blast it—if you love me, why were you going off with Danvers?'

'I wasn't! I didn't even know he'd be coming with Donald Ogg. Anyway, *you* were the one who was threatening to leave.'

'Only because I wanted you to ask me to stay!'

Tearful laughter bubbled inside her as she clasped her arms tightly round his neck and gave him an unsteady smile. 'You really are impossible, you know that? Do you think you can stop growling at me long enough to kiss me? Please?'

She leaned forward, her mouth meeting his in an explosive kiss that made her head spin. Now that she had found him she would never let him go again. She pressed her lips down the line of his jaw until her face was buried in the warm brown curve of his throat and she could hear the swift thud of his heart echoing hers. 'Please stay,' she sighed, holding him with all her strength. 'I need you, Kyle.'

'Then why didn't you say so before, you little idiot?' he breathed in her ear. 'That's all I wanted to hear.'

Very slowly, he let her feet down to touch the ground and then he drew her fully against him, one arm wrapped around her waist while the other hand tipped her chin up. His gaze ran hungrily across her flushed face as he bent to touch his lips to hers, tenderly at first, then with a soaring passion that made her press closer, every inch of her body responding to the longing she felt in him.

When he lifted his head at last, she stared breathlessly up at him, amazed by the things he had told her without words. 'How long have you felt this way?'

'Ages,' he confessed with a rueful smile. 'Certainly since the day you stood in the cave bristling and swearing to fight me if I tried to sell Drumm. After that I stopped trying to get rid of you because I knew you cared about Drumm as much as I did. And besides, I discovered I didn't want you to leave.'

'Couldn't you have told me that?' she demanded.

'I intended to. But I thought it was wiser to let the dust settle first—to give you a chance to forget about the way I'd been behaving. And then that flaming Danvers arrived! I was furious that he'd used his friendship with you to get close to the long barrow, but I was jealous as hell, too.'

'But you went rushing off to see Morag!' she exclaimed.

A sheepish smile touched his lips. 'You mean that's what I told Mrs McTavish. It was a puerile attempt to get back at you, but I couldn't relax for thinking of you with Danvers, and when I did get back and found him kissing you it was too much. There I'd been curbing my own feelings for three solid weeks and you had the gall to taunt me about self-control. Good grief, I'd been deliberately keeping my distance!'

'You didn't keep your distance in Edinburgh,' she reminded him softly, moving her body provocatively against his.

'I remember.' His eyes had darkened with desire as he clasped her more closely. 'I don't know what Morag told you, but I never proposed marriage to her. I knew that all she ever saw in me was the prospect of a fortune when Hamish died. When she turned up in Edinburgh I told her it was all over between us and she'd better stop making trouble. Then I came to find you—because I was genuinely concerned about you.'

'And I misunderstood,' Ilona sighed. 'I was so mixed-up about you. Oh, I've made so many mistakes, Kyle. Forgive me, please.'

For answer he kissed her with an aching tenderness that made all her bones feel jellified; then he laid his forehead on hers, looking deep into her eyes. 'I love you very much,' he told her, his voice deep and vibrant. 'Lord knows I've asked you often enough, but maybe this time you'll believe me ... Marry me, Ilona. Marry me right away.'

'Right away?' she queried, a catch in her throat.

'As soon as possible. Let's have an island wedding. We'll open up the old kirk and invite everyone to come.'

'Will you wear the kilt?' she asked with dancing eyes.

'On Drumm,' he replied with mock solemnity, 'the bridegroom always wears the kilt. But the bride doesn't wear the trousers.'

'No bride of yours would dare,' she laughed, filled with heady joy. 'Oh, Kyle, if only Hamish had invited me to visit him sooner! We might have met and fallen in love without the hassle.'

'Think so?' he asked with a grin. 'Oh, we shall go on having hassles, my love. I've got a filthy temper, I warn you.'

'It goes with your hair,' she teased, rumpling the errant red curls.

'I'm afraid so. Can you put up with it?'

Head on one side, she pretended to consider that, but she was smiling and warm messages passed between them as they stood close together. 'Think what fun we'll have making up,' she said. 'Anyway, I don't think I'd enjoy living with a tame man. You're perfect just the way you are—a little bit wild. My beautiful Viking.'

'My lovely mermaid,' he returned, drawing her even closer as he kissed her again.

Much later, when Ilona remembered Hugh and Donald, she glanced down at the loch and saw the boat drawn up on the grass with her cases beside it, but of the two men there was no sign.

'We must have convinced them there was no need to stay,' said Kyle, tucking his arm round her waist. 'Let's go and get your luggage.'

Arms around each other, they set off down the hill, pausing every few steps to exchange more sweet kisses.

'Alice McVeigh will be disappointed the legend didn't work out the way she predicted,' he remarked as he picked up her belongings.

'She only said there was something fateful in store for you,' Ilona replied. 'And she was right—you're going to be a married man. But, Kyle, what are you going to do about Morag?'

'I've already done it—packed her off to go back on the provision boat, the way she arrived. I wish I'd never run into her last night—if I hadn't been feeling so low, I'd never have mentioned that I might be leaving Drumm. However, we shan't be seeing her again. I'm afraid I was extremely rude to her half an hour ago.'

She walked beside him back up the hill to where the helicopter waited, saying eventually, 'Do you really think faithfulness is an outdated concept?'

'Did I say that?' he asked, round-eyed and teasing her. 'Let me catch you flirting with some other man and you'll soon find out how I feel about that subject. You shouldn't take me so seriously when I'm being pigheaded.'

'Pigheaded as a mule,' she smiled, remembering the housekeeper's quaint turn of phrase. 'Which reminds me—Mrs McTavish said we were blethering idiots. I think she must have guessed how we felt.'

'She certainly knew how *I* felt,' he replied. 'Apparently when I was feverish all I did was rave about how much I wanted you.'

'Is that why she wouldn't let me near you?'

'Probably. Didn't want me embarrassing you, I expect.'

As he stowed her cases into the helicopter, Ilona said mischievously, 'Then when you said you loved me and dragged me into bed with you that morning, you did know who I was?'

Kyle stared at her, thunderstruck. 'When I did what?'

'Oh, I'll tell you about that later,' she said with a laugh, lifting on tiptoe to kiss him before skipping away round the machine to climb aboard and strap herself in. 'Come on, Mr Lachlan. Let's go home!'

Here is a selection of Mills & Boon novels to be published at about the same time as the book you are reading.

£5.25 net each